# What Dreams
# May Come

*By Manly Wade Wellman*

WHAT DREAMS MAY COME
THE HANGING STONES
THE LOST AND THE LURKING
AFTER DARK
THE OLD GODS WAKEN

# What Dreams May Come

MANLY WADE WELLMAN

DOUBLEDAY & COMPANY, INC.

GARDEN CITY, NEW YORK

1983

All of the characters in this book
are fictitious and any resemblance
to actual persons, living or dead,
is purely coincidental.

*Library of Congress Cataloging in Publication Data*
Wellman, Manly Wade, 1905–
What dreams may come.
I. Title.
PS3545.E52858W48   1983      813'.54

ISBN: 0-385-18253-8
Library of Congress Catalog Card Number 82-40399
Copyright © 1983 by Manly Wade Wellman

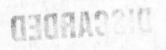

# Foreword

Manifestly there is an England and, as Englishmen earnestly assure us, there always will be. And in London, in Herbrand Street, there is actually a public house called the Friend at Hand, much praised and prized by its numerous clientele. It may be further worthwhile to point out that various books herein noticed, by Richard Leakey, Alexander Marshack, Anne Moberly and Eleanor Jourdain, John Pfeiffer, Gene Stuart, and Ruth St. Leger-Gordon, also are real and readable and may be found in the larger libraries.

But no such community as Claines exists in England, or, so far as I can ascertain, anywhere else in the known world. And the names, physical aspects, behaviors, and motivations of men and women represented as present in the houses and streets of Claines are wholly imaginary, though it is earnestly to be hoped that they seem convincing.

*Manly Wade Wellman*
Chapel Hill, North Carolina, 1983

# What Dreams
# May Come

*From realms of viewless spirits tears the veil,*
*And half reveals the unutterable tale . . .*
Matthew Gregory Lewis, *Tales of Terror*

# CHAPTER 1

The motor bus from London, silver-gray with maroon trim, purred westward across the broad concrete bridge. Below crept a wide, murky stream. The summer afternoon sunlight was golden. The bus slowed as it ran between two sprawls of houses. At the right stood a compact little church of drab stone, crowned with a steeple. Beyond that, low store buildings to the right, dwellings of various sizes to the left. On the far side of the leftward scatter of homes climbed a steep slope, grassy and tufted with scrubby bushes. Flung upon it was a vast white figure like a squat, misshapen man, made by digging the turf from the chalk beneath.

The bus rolled into a paved parking lot in front of a squat brick structure that bore a great square signboard labeled THE MOONRAVEN. Under the name was pictured a round disc of pale yellow, upon which soared the lean black silhouette of a flying bird, like a shallow V. The bus stopped next to two small cars.

"Here's Claines, sir," said the driver, and John Thunstone rose from the front seat at the left.

He looked tall and massive in the aisle as he put big hands to the rack overhead and hoisted down a big suitcase and a smaller one. He wore a finely fitted dark jacket and striped trousers. On his well-combed dark head slanted a tweed hat. A raincoat draped itself on his cliff like shoulder. Under one arm he tucked a walking stick of blotched brown wood with a silver band several inches below the curved handle. His serious face was square, with a streak of closely trimmed mustache. His nose had a dint where once it had been broken.

"Thank you," he said, tramping to the door and out.

"And thank you, sir," said the driver, levering the door shut again.

Thunstone glanced at the watch on his wrist. It was a quarter to three. Then he stood and gazed up the slope beyond the hamlet there to the south, at the grotesque white figure silhouetted upon it. After a moment, he carried his suitcases to the door of the Moonraven, shouldered it open and entered upon a floor of wide planks, and crossed to the bar at the back. Sitting on a stool, he told a plump woman behind the bar, "A half of bitter, please."

"Ahf of bitter, right you are, sir."

She filled a glass mug at a tap. Thunstone put a pound note on the bar and sipped at his drink. "I hope to stay in Claines for a few days," he said to the woman.

As he spoke, he looked around the barroom. It was neatly paneled in buff-colored wood, with rafters streaking the ceiling overhead. To one side was set a sort of counter with shelves, on which were dishes and pans. Tables stood here and there. Under the windows at the front were ranged trestles with benches. Half a dozen customers communed with their drinks. Thunstone liked the look of the place.

"Perhaps you're here on business, sir," ventured the woman at the bar.

"Well, more or less to visit, to look at things," said Thunstone. "Such as that figure up on the hill beyond your town."

"I take it you're American, sir. But here's my husband, he can tell you more about that there picture up in the chalk, what they call Old Thunder."

A customer had fetched his mug to the bar, and she went away to refill it. A man in a tawny jacket had strolled to where Thunstone sat. This was a middle-sized, middle-aged man, with a round, good-humored face.

"So you're interested in our little place here, sir?" he greeted Thunstone. "We like it, though it's small even for a village. More like what you'd call a hamlet. Elwain Hawes is my name. I'm landlord of the Moonraven, Mr.—"

"Thunstone." They shook hands. "I'm more or less of an antiquarian; I look into historic and prehistoric curiosities. I came here on impulse because I heard in London about Claines and your figure on the hill. Mrs. Hawes said it's called Old Thunder. What is it, anyway?"

"Ah, what indeed? You may well ask, Mr. Thunstone. All that can be truly said is, it's been there from before what can be remembered. It was made up there, I daresay, by the old heathen folk long centuries back; maybe they worshipped it after their manner. And each year this time, the people clear away the turf to show it clear in outline. Parson—our curate, Mr. Gates up at the church, St. Jude's—he's tried in his time to study it out. He just might answer your questions."

"I plan to make a stay here for a few days," Thunstone said again. "Do you have accommodations here?"

"Regret to say, Mr. Thunstone, we're not fitted up for lodgings. What we get in here is just the local folk and daytime travelers. But right across Trail Street from us here, Mrs. Fothergill can give you bed and breakfast. I've been told she does well by those who come to her. And here at the Moonraven, we do people a lunch—buffet style—" He nodded toward the counter. "Oo, cold ham, cold beef, sausages, Scotch eggs, salads. A goodish crowd most noons, lorry and van drivers like to stop, and local residents. Likewise at dinnertime, what we call an ordinary for those as are disposed to take it. A cut off the joint and veg and so on. Plain, I'm afraid, but we think well cooked."

"Plain and well cooked," said Thunstone after him, and smiled. "That sounds all right to me, Mr. Hawes."

He finished the last of his bitter, picked up his change, and rose.

"All right," he said. "I'll do as you suggest, go over to Mrs. Fothergill's and see if I can get a room there. And I'd like to come back here for more talk later."

"Thank you, sir. It'll be a fair pleasure."

Thunstone took his cane, powerfully hoisted his suitcases, and walked out. He crossed the parking lot and stopped at the edge of the paved street. Three or four cars trundled past, then a dark red truck-and-trailer combination. A tall, spare young policeman rode a bicycle along. Thunstone gazed across to a two-story house, sturdily clapboarded and painted white. Flowers grew along the foundations. To one side rose a tree, so festooned with ivy that it was unidentifiable as to species. A huge rectangle of a sign rose against a pillar of the porch. Even at that distance, he could read the big letters plainly:

BED &

BREAKFAST

MRS. ALMA FOTHERGILL, PROP.

He waited for a moment when the traffic thinned out both ways, and carried his luggage across. He mounted broad stone steps to the front door. It had a pane of stained glass and a placard, COME IN.

Thunstone came in, to a narrow, shadowed hallway with a staircase mounting upward at the left side. From the rear of the house, someone appeared. "Yes, sir?" said a low, vibrating voice.

"I was told I might get lodging here," said Thunstone.

"Yes, of course." It was an upstanding woman with a lofty swirl of shiny fair hair. She wore a figured blue frock, not fitted to her but softly draped to accent a full, rich figure. She smiled. Her teeth were white, her wide lips were painted red, her round face pinkly made up. She was in her forties as Thunstone guessed, and making the deliberate most of herself.

He set down his suitcases and took off his hat. Fine streaks of gray showed in his carefully parted black hair.

"Of course," she made a rather singing two words of it. "We can provide you with bed and breakfast." She seemed to be consciously affecting an educated accent. "For how long will you stay?" she asked.

"I can't exactly say, but I think for several days. I've just arrived in Claines. What are your charges?"

She told him the charges, and Thunstone said they were reasonable. "This way if you please," she said, and led him into the hall.

She moved up the stairs lightly for so big a woman. She winnowed as she ascended. The hall above was lighted by a window at the front.

"My name is Mrs. Fothergill," she told him. "Mrs. Alma Fothergill. Here—" and she opened a darkly varnished door. "Might this suit you?"

The room was perhaps twelve feet square, papered with a scramble of roses. Next to its single window at the side of the house stood a bed with a massive wooden headboard and a spread with the pale, puffy look of oatmeal porridge. Above the bed hung a hooded electric light. There was an armchair, a small desk with a straight chair, a bureau and mirror, a stand that held a glass carafe of water and a glass. Thunstone studied a framed oil painting of two cows knee-deep in a tree-fringed pond.

"Do you like that picture, Mr.—"

"Thunstone," he supplied.

"Yes, Mr. Thunstone, that was painted by a cousin of mine. Dear Osbert. And is the room satisfactory?"

"Yes, indeed." Thunstone set his suitcases at the foot of the bed, draped his raincoat upon them, and tossed his hat on top. "I expect to be comfortable here."

She smiled with her china-white teeth. "There's a bath at the far end of the hall—hot and cold water and a shower. As of just now, you're our only guest, though I get people going through—a good lot of backpackers hiking here and there, for instance. Such nice people. Now, if you'll come down and sign the register."

He left his hat but brought his cane. Downstairs, she led him into a front parlor with plants slung in pots at the windows and china dogs and ducks on the mantel of the fireplace. A rolltop desk was there, with a yellow pencil upon it. Against the wall stood a sideboard with an array of bottles. Thunstone sat down and wrote his name and his New York address, then the address of his hotel on Southampton Row in London. Mrs. Fothergill looked over his shoulder.

"An American gentleman," she said, in tones of approval. "Now and then I have Americans here, and they're an interesting, attractive lot. You know," and she rolled her blue eyes a trifle, "I don't truly need to operate here for B-and-B. I've a good lot laid by at interest— my dear husband's insurance, and Dad and Mum left me something, too. But I like the company I get. I like best the ones from foreign parts, such as you. Like to talk with them. Meet new people, hear of new customs, and so on."

He finished his writing. "Captain John Smith said something like that once."

"Captain John Smith? Oh, he was in America, I believe."

"Yes. Now, let me pay for tonight and tomorrow night for the present, and I'll see how much longer my stay will last."

He took a billfold from the inside of his pocket and gave her some notes.

"Thank you." She opened a drawer in the desk, put the money in a metal box inside, and locked the drawer. Then she gestured toward an arched doorway at the rear of the parlor.

"That's the breakfast room in there. We serve breakfast at eight o'clock in the morning, unless you would want it later."

"Eight o'clock will suit me, Mrs. Fothergill," Thunstone assured her. "I don't want you to make yourself too busy on my account."

"But it's never hard to do things when you have a system." Again her smile. "I do well here, though I say it myself. I bring a man to work in the yard, do repairs now and then, and I've a girl back in the kitchen. She's not really a servant; she's a young friend who lives with me here and helps me. I'm grateful for that help. And speaking of help," she went on, with even more of a smile, "if I may ask, is there any help we might give you in whatever you plan to do here?"

She had sat herself down to ask that. Apparently she liked to talk to him. She had crossed one knee over the other, showing plump calves in fawn-colored stockings. Her feet were small, and wore high-heeled blue sandals strapped at the slim ankles. Thunstone looked back at her, and decided that the bright yellow of her hair had skillful treatment from a hairdresser. It reminded him of orange marmalade. He wondered if there was a hairdresser in as small a community as Claines. Perhaps she went regularly to a beauty shop in the neighboring factory and market town of Gerrinsford, through which the bus had brought him here. That would be a journey of seven or eight miles every few weeks.

"I'm glad to talk about why I came," Thunstone said easily. "I'm a student of antiquities and customs, and I was in London to look into some publications at the library of the British Museum. I have some English friends who spoke about Claines. About a fallen pillar of stone, and that figure, cut out to the chalk on the hill above us here."

"Oh, ah," she said, nodding. "Sweepside, we call that rise of ground. It belongs to Mr. Ensley at Chimney Pots. Old Thunder, yes;

though I don't know how that name came to be given. It seems to always have been called that. I should say that I was brought up in Claines, here in this very house. But then I grew up and went to London." She stirred, as though to preen herself. "I was on the stage, you see."

"I see," said Thunstone, who did not feel great surprise to hear that she had been on the stage.

"And then I married in London. But my husband died—he was a photographer, an art photographer. And when my dear father and mother died, too, four years ago, I returned here." Her blue eyes studied him. "But enough about me. You're an antiquarian, you said."

"In a modest way, yes, I am."

"That sounds so interesting. And Mrs. Thunstone, has she come to England with you?"

"There's no Mrs. Thunstone."

At that she brightened and smiled again. She seemed ready to giggle, but did not.

"May I sit here for a minute or so and make some notes?" he asked.

"Why yes, of course. But excuse me for an instant."

She rose and winnowed out.

Thunstone fished a loose-leaf notebook from the side pocket of his jacket and uncapped a ballpoint pen. At the top of a page he wrote the date, *Thursday, July 1,* and below that wrote the things he had heard from Hawes at the Moonraven and Mrs. Fothergill. Some words he underscored. As he finished writing, Mrs. Fothergill returned. She bore a silver tray, and on it a silver teapot and cups and a plate of small cakes.

"It's four o'clock, or nearly," she said, "and I like an early tea if there's time. I thought you might care to join me, Mr. Thunstone."

"You're very kind," he said, rising to take the tray and put it on a small side table. "And maybe you'll let me ask some more questions."

"If I can answer any of them." She poured the tea. "Cream?" she asked him. "Sugar?"

"No, thank you."

She handed him a cup and a small plate with a frosted currant cake and a paper napkin decorated with cupids. He sipped. "This is very good," he praised the tea.

"And good of you to say so. I don't think that many Americans appreciate tea."

"We appreciate it so little that once we threw a whole shipload of it into Boston Harbor."

She laughed at that, perhaps more than the joke deserved. "Can I help you with what you want to know about Claines, then?" she asked.

"I hope you can." Teacup in one hand, pen in the other, he looked at her. "I mean the pillar of stone. I heard it said that every year, about this time, the people turn it over where it lies. Do you know why?"

"Oh, ah," she said again. "Yes, that does happen, but as to why, I'm afraid I can't hazard a guess. I only know that it's gone on, year after year, since ever there was a Claines, as I suppose."

He wrote down what she said. "And how long has there been a Claines?" he asked.

"Forever, more or less. Our curate here at St. Jude's, young Mr. Gates, he might have a date of some sort."

"I've heard his name," said Thunstone.

"They do say that Mr. Gates wants to write some sort of history of Claines. And too, he might speak to that fallen pillar; it's called the Dream Rock. It so happens that it lies at the edge of the St. Jude's churchyard. You could ask Mr. Gates, and I'm sure he'd talk to you."

Thunstone drank the rest of his tea. He finished writing, closed the notebook and put it in his pocket, and rose.

"Thank you for giving me tea," he said. "You've been very hospitable, Mrs. Fothergill."

"Not at all."

"Now, if you'll excuse me, I'll go walk about the town for a while."

Cane in hand, he went into the hall and out at the front door, aware that she watched him go. He had a sense that something else watched, and wondered if that was a fancy.

# CHAPTER 2

Bareheaded, Thunstone paused on the sidewalk. He leaned slightly on his cane and allowed himself a moment to look at what he could see of Claines.

On his side of the street were homes. Two of them stood east of Mrs. Fothergill's, two small, respectable-looking little cottages. On beyond these rose a structure of some size.

It was of sooty-looking gray stone, it seemed to have a battlement above its front, and several chimneys ranged along the roof. Mrs. Fothergill had spoken of a place called Chimney Pots. Probably he was looking at it. He waited for a lull in motor traffic, walked quickly across Trail Street, and turned right in front of the Moonraven to continue along in front of the business houses.

They were, understandably, modest business houses. The Moonraven looked large in comparison with most of them. Thunstone strolled past a little cabin of a shop that proclaimed itself Post Office, but displayed postcards and boxes of candy in its window, then past another that promised Fish & Chips, then a larger one with long glass display windows and big letters above them, LUDLAM'S MARKET. A little alley ran beyond Ludlam's, and across Trail Street became a gravel-strewn cross street. Along that way on the far side Thunstone could see more homes, a sort of handful of them. Some were of the sort called workmen's cottages. Several larger ones with two stories probably were divided into small flats. Across the alley he paused again, in front of a gloomy place with a broad, open doorway and the information GARAGE & MACHINE SHOP, A. PORRASK. A massive man in stained overalls stood beside the gasoline pump—petrol pump, they would call it here in England—tightening something with a screwdriver. He turned and glowered at Thunstone with flinty eyes in a black-bearded face.

"Yus?" he croaked. "What is it?"

"I'm just walking along," said Thunstone, and did so. The flinty eyes looked with disfavor at the silver-banded cane he swung.

Snuggled close to Porrask's enterprise was a pub smaller and shabbier than the Moonraven. Its sign called it THE WAGGONER. Two men lounged there, presumably waiting for it to open at five o'clock. The policeman Thunstone had seen before brought his bicycle close and stopped, one foot on the pavement.

"Pardon me, Officer," Thunstone said. "Can you give me some information?"

"If I have it, sir." He was a young, rangy man with a long face and a heavy, neat brown mustache. "Do you mean, about Claines?"

"Yes, I'm here on a visit. Over across the street, is that the place called Chimney Pots?"

Both of them looked across. From that point, Thunstone had a good view. It was a massive building of rough, gloomy rock, that held bits of light, like sparks in dying coals. There were heavily framed windows above and below, a wide porch with pillars. The assembly of broad chimneys on the roof were each crowned with cylindrical pots.

"Yes, sir, that's called Chimney Pots," said the policeman. "The owner is Mr. Gram Ensley, who owns a good deal of property here."

The policeman's accent was what Thunstone had heard called an educated one. His manner was cordial, though official.

"You're well acquainted here?" suggested Thunstone.

"It's my business to be, though I'm not from here. I was born in Newcastle; I went to college at Reading. When I joined the force, they assigned me to Claines."

"I see," said Thunstone. "Now, I'd like to meet Mr. Gates, the minister here."

"Yes, sir—Father Gates, he'd like to be called, though he's a curate as yet, not a rector. This is a Thursday, and I'd look for him to be in his study at the church, there on ahead. St. Jude's, that is."

"Thank you, Officer."

Thunstone walked on toward the church. He had only glanced at it on the bus coming into Claines. At second glance, it was not a large church, nor yet a particularly impressive one. It had been built of smudgy-looking stone and was square and flat-roofed, with a small steeple to relieve the monotony of its architecture. At the side was a cemetery, dotted with small drab tombstones. A hedge ran around this except at the side next to the street. There lay a long, worn obelisk, grubbily pale, with grass tufted all around it. Thunstone walked to it and leaned lightly on his cane to study it.

The thing was eight feet or more in length, roughly rounded, and perhaps two and a half feet through at its largest diameter. Some kind of schist, judged Thunstone. He bent to see more closely. It had been shaped at some time or other, perhaps to simulate a human form, but what might have been shoulders had dwindled away with time. The top of the obelisk was, or had been, a roughly head like knob. On the surface of the rock were the traces of markings. They might have been deeply incised at one time, but years of wear and weather had reduced them to faintness.

A shadow fell at Thunstone's feet, and he turned to look.

He had been joined by a youngish man almost as tall and sturdy as himself, dressed in dark clericals. The resolute-jawed face looked gravely curious. It was crowned with thick brown hair, closely curled. Deep blue eyes questioned Thunstone.

"I believe you must be the Reverend Mr. Gates," said Thunstone. "I'm a visitor in Claines; Thunstone's my name. And this," he set the tip of his cane to the obelisk, "must be what they call the Dream Rock."

"Yes," said Gates, "that's the Dream Rock, right enough."

Thunstone felt a tremor in the hand that held the cane, something like a minor electric shock. He drew the cane away, and the tremor in his hand went away.

"The Dream Rock," repeated Gates, "and it's a bad dream where I'm concerned." He looked at Thunstone. "I read folklore and anti-quarian magazines, and your name is familiar to me. You have an appreciation of things. What's your reaction to the Dream Rock?"

"When I touched it with my cane just now, I had a sensation like an electric current running up my arm."

"Really?" said Gates. "It's an evil rock, that. It survives from times of arrant paganism. Well, Mr. Thunstone, I'm glad that you came along."

"A very intelligent young policeman directed me to you."

"That would be young Constable Dymock," Gates said. "In a way, he's coming along as I'm coming along. We both won university scholarships—he to Reading, I to Oxford. We both knew what careers we wanted; he wanted criminology, I wanted religion. I rather like Dymock. We've begun more or less together in Claines."

Gates looked Thunstone up and down.

"If you have a few minutes, you might like to come to my study and tell me what you think of Claines."

"I'll be glad of the chance to talk to you," Thunstone assured him.

Gates led Thunstone along a flagged walk to the church and around it to a handsomely cleated door of stained oak, then through that to a room lighted by two windows. Gates's study was not of the tidiest, but Thunstone thought it was interesting. An inner wall was given over to shelves of books, clear up to the ceiling. There was a desk of pale wood, with papers and a typewriter and an empty teacup. Gates motioned Thunstone to an armchair and seated himself at the desk. His movements were easy but powerful.

"You say you felt a sort of current when you touched the Dream Rock with your cane," he said. "That's a rather interesting cane, if I may say so."

"It's a sword cane," said Thunstone.

"Is it, indeed?"

"I'll show you."

Thunstone turned the handle around and cleared the blade inside. It slid out of the hollowed shank. It shone palely. He passed it over to Gates, who took it carefully and narrowed his deep-set blue eyes to study it.

"A silver blade," he said. "And there's an inscription on it." His eyes became slits as he peered. "Latin," he said after a moment, and read aloud: *"Sic pereant omnes inimici tui, Domine.* Yes, from the Psalms. 'So perish all thine enemies, O God.' "

"The man who gave it to me says it was forged by Saint Dunstan, a thousand years ago."

Gates was deeply impressed. "I've never seen anything like it," he said.

He passed the sword back, and Thunstone sheathed it in the shank of the cane. "There happens to be at least one other like it," he said. "That one belongs to my friend Judge Keith Hilary Pursuivant. He gave me this. But let me say that what interests me about you, Father, is that you're supposed to be working toward a history of this interesting little town."

"This little hamlet," Gates said, using the same word that Hawes had used at the Moonraven. "I should explain first why I happen to be here. I came as a curate to the parish at Gerrinsford, which includes Claines. But there's a bequest, a very old bequest, that provides for St. Jude's to be kept active, and so my vicar assigned me here. I'm not a true vicar as yet."

He spoke as though he wanted to be a true vicar, and Thunstone said, "That will follow, I'd think."

"I hope so. I've done some articles on church matters that have attracted attention, and I have encouragement about the publication of my history of Claines."

"I've already called Claines an interesting town," offered Thunstone.

"We call it a hamlet because it isn't truly a town," said Gates. "We haven't a mayor or any local government. No police department except Constable Dymock. And we aren't a parish; we have just St. Jude's and myself as curate. We don't have even a great house."

"How about Chimney Pots?" Thunstone asked.

"Oh," and Gates smiled, "a pleasant place enough, but hardly a stately home of England. Have you been to any of those?"

"To a couple, with coach tours," Thunstone told him. "Frankly, I felt like an intruder when I walked in. Of course, I was making certain studies."

"Certain studies," Gates echoed. "If I may hazard a guess, you're a university man."

"Not exactly," said Thunstone, shaking his dark head. "I went to a small southern college—Carrington—because I could get some modest financial help if I played football there. After that, I took some graduate courses at Columbia in New York City and at the University of North Carolina, but no degree at either school."

"You say you played American football," said Gates.

"I was a center. That's not a particularly glorious position."

"Is that anywhere near as violent a game as rugby? I played footer in public school, but I only boxed for my university."

"From what I've seen of English football," said Thunstone, "I'd hazard a guess that if you got into the American game in the gear you wear here, you'd be lucky to live two minutes." He changed the subject. "But you said that you're writing a history of Claines."

"That is correct. It's a small place, but its history is a long one."

As Gates told it, it was a long history. Nobody could be sure how old Claines might be as a community. All that records could be made to show was that some sort of settlement had existed there since Roman times, and occasional digs and probings—it was hard for scholars to get permission to dig, it seemed—revealed that people had lived there in pre-Roman times, yes, even back to the Stone Age. Flint points had been turned up there, the sort of things that country people called elf arrows and even saw as weapons of supernatural force. And in medieval days, armed bands of rival lords had skirmished back and forth there.

But Claines, though so old, had never grown large. That, said Gates, was because it had never truly had room to grow. It stood on a sort of hummock of turfy ground, bounded in by marsh and fen. An example of that bounding was the turbid stream over which Thunstone had come in the bus, which bore the uninviting name of Congdon Mire. There might be three hundred residents or so, most of them employed in nearby Gerrinsford in factories and offices. There were a few sheep keepers and market gardeners. They lived in Claines, it seemed, because they had no wish or will to live anywhere else.

"That big slope of ground they call Sweepside," said Thunstone. "With the figure they call Old Thunder. I'd expect it to be a promising place for archaeological exploration."

"Perhaps so," said Gates, "but it belongs to Mr. Gram Ensley, who owns Chimney Pots. Who also owns and lets out most of the houses in Claines. Mr. Ensley is fairly stubborn about allowing investigation on his land. One group of antiquarians got stubborn, too, and he got a court injunction against their coming. And he declined to talk to two different enterprises who wanted to build factories on Sweepside. He won't even rent land on Sweepside to people who would like to have market gardens there. He has flocks of sheep, and they graze there, and that's all."

"What about the residents here?"

"A decent lot they are, for the most part," Gates summed up. "Claines might have been absorbed into Gerrinsford long ago except for the intervening swampiness, but it has stayed a backwater, and it has its individuality. People work hard, in Gerrinsford places or on what land they have, and they're glad to be decently quiet at home after dinner. Oh, the young men and women may get on the bus and see a film in town, or otherwise amuse themselves there, but their fathers and mothers are content to sit and watch the telly if they can afford one. Some have the telly without truly being able to afford it. And this little church of ours is a factor," Gates went on, brightening. "Always good attendance at services, and we have programs and festivals from time to time. And a group of church ladies is active, visiting the sick, helping unfortunate poor families."

Gates paused, frowning. Thunstone waited for him to continue. He continued:

"If I could turn a certain element from what must be considered ancient paganism—ancient sorcery." He gestured with a broad hand. "Up there on Sweepside, this very day, they're hard at it cleaning the chalky lines of their superstitious Old Thunder figure."

"And this Mr. Ensley won't let scholars explore there."

"Not he. He's posted Sweepside. Nobody can go there without his permission. Though he allows the work on Old Thunder."

"What sort of man is he?"

"Courteous enough, I must admit. He doesn't attend church often, but from time to time he makes a contribution. A substantial contribution. Otherwise, he keeps to himself most of the time. He might talk to you. Like me, he's interested in Claines, and well he might be. He owns so much of it, both sides of Trail Street."

"Why is it called Trail Street?" was Thunstone's next question.

"Because there must have been a trail there before there was a street, I should think. An old Roman road was traced along it by some survey or other. And a Roman road was apt to have followed a road of people older than Romans."

"That's an interesting thought," commented Thunstone. He wrote busily, and again Gates narrowed his eyes to watch.

"See here, Mr. Thunstone," said Gates after a moment. "I'm going to ask you a cheeky question, and you can answer it or not just as you wish. Are you here in some sort of official capacity?"

Thunstone laughed easily as he wrote. "Not in the least. I came to England to do some private research into England's remote past. I've been to Stonehenge, Avebury, and so on. I've spent time in the libraries at Oxford and Cambridge, and at the British Museum in London. You said you'd seen some things I've written in folklore journals, so perhaps you know what I'm looking for. When I heard a mention of Claines, I came here more or less on impulse. I'm particularly interested in what you call the Dream Rock out there. You feel that it's pagan."

"It was pagan, right enough," said Gates, shaking his head. "What chiefly disturbs me is the annual turning and what attends it. Midnight, and people hallooing and doing a sort of dance, right next to the church. It's like a witches' Sabbath."

Thunstone had seen witches' Sabbaths in his time, but forbore to say so. "And you'd like to stop it," he prompted.

"I would indeed. The night of the annual turning is this coming Sunday, July 4—your own special holiday in America. And it's also the third Sunday after Trinity. At morning prayer that day, I propose to deliver a strong sermon against paganism and sorcery." His heavy hand touched a stack of scribbled papers on the desk. "I invite you to come to church and hear it."

"I'll be glad to do that." Thunstone rose and tucked his notebook into his pocket. "And perhaps we can talk further about Claines—about ancient paganism, too—when you have time."

"It would be a pleasure, sir."

Gates rose and saw him out.

Thunstone walked back toward the center of the little business district. He savored the pleasant mildness of the bright afternoon. The first day of July here was more like the middle of May at home in America. England was so far north, he reminded himself; without the warm Gulf Stream to cuddle it, England might be subarctic. England had been subarctic, not too many thousands of years ago.

He paused to stand and gaze up the street and down. This was England, he reflected, this little community called a hamlet by Hawes and Gates because it was not large enough to be called a village; Claines, this strew of houses along a main thoroughfare called Trail Street—Trail, as though it ran through a wilderness.

For England was like this. Like this everywhere, the small as well as the great. Great London was an English marvel. Samuel Johnson had said to Boswell that when a man was tired of London he was tired of life. Johnson had been right, as usually he had been right about things. But London, for all its Englishness, was also international. It could be all things to foreigners as to Englishmen. Thunstone had heard a friend say bitterly that London was no longer a white man's town, one who in saying that had sounded like the diehard, death-or-glory voice of the Empire that now was no more. Without agreeing, Thunstone saw what his friend had meant about throngs of swarthy people speaking in strange tongues. Away here in Claines, with nothing to bring strangers, there were no strangers except for himself. There were only the English.

All the more English because the houses were mostly small, matter-of-fact, here and there even shabby. Because along Trail Street were only a few modest shops, the Moonraven pub where buses stopped, the post office, Ludlam's store, the fish-and-chips cubicle, the garage with the surly-looking man with the beard. Upon Claines the antiquity of England somehow rested, like the hem of a strangely figured mantle wrought long ago.

Trail Street, so named, Gates had felt, because it must have been a trail before it ever was a street. Along it, perhaps, pilgrims had trotted their horses eastward toward London and the Tabard Inn where they would join Geoffrey Chaucer and the Knight and the sweet Prioress and the Miller and the buxom Wife of Bath for the pilgrimage to Canterbury. Before those had been cross-gartered, wheat-bearded Saxons, not yet whipped in battle by the Normans and by them willy-nilly refined, taught new words, new laws. Before the Saxons, Roman legionaries with shining helmets and shields and javelins, on their invading march in or their abandoning way out. And yet before them, before even the Celts, those dimly defined first Britons, those chippers of stone, those who must have cut down to the chalk on Sweepside to outline the figure of whatever god or hero or monster it was that today the people of Claines called Old Thunder.

This was England because England had been England so long, could not be wholly smothered out by modern matters. England was immemorial, and immemorially alive and mighty. Thunstone's America was mighty, too. He loved America. America was ancient. But you couldn't know ancient America, could only vaguely imagine America before those four brief centuries of the overlay of civilization which now was America.

That overlay, and the heritage of what had been America before it. You ate corn, you smoked tobacco, you paddled a canoe, you lounged in a hammock. Yes, and if you plowed a field you sometimes turned up stone arrowheads, beautifully chipped into graceful points. Just as here in England, sometimes the share turned up a stone point, amazingly like the ones in America. In such things as those, America and England had a facet of agreement, the stone implements of vanished tribes. Lost things found again, making you turn your face to look back upon unknown beginnings.

He might be the only foreigner just now in Claines, but he was not truly a foreigner, because he saw and felt things so vividly.

He looked across Trail Street at a very small cottage, hardly larger than a tool shed. In the yard stood a sign, POLICE STATION, and by the doorstep stood Dymock, the policeman he had met earlier, of whom Gates had spoken sympathetically. His helmet was off, and he held a china mug in his hand and sipped from it. On impulse, Thunstone strolled across and into the yard.

"Yes, sir?" said Dymock. "Anything wrong, sir?"

"Not a thing," Thunstone assured him. "You sent me to Mr. Gates, and he spoke about you in a way that made me feel I'd like to be better acquainted."

"He spoke of me?" Dymock asked above his mug.

"Yes, and quite cordially. He said that you and he were somewhat alike. Both university men, and both called to fine careers—he to uphold Christian faith, you to uphold the law. And that both of you had come here to Claines, in hopes of advancement in your careers."

"That's kind of him," said Dymock. A smile twitched his mustache. "Yes, I always wanted to do police work, and after I graduated at Reading I took criminology courses at Hendon. I hope to get into the CID, all that. But they start you out at the bottom, and let you find your own way up from there."

"The bottom," said Thunstone after him. "In the police department at Claines."

Dymock smiled again. "I'm the whole police department in Claines, the one constable on duty here. I daresay that makes me the chief, and the whole force as well."

It was a new notion to Thunstone. "You make it sound as if you're always on duty."

"Well, yes, I suppose I am. When I'm needed, wherever I'm needed. If more is needed than just myself, Gerrinsford will send over help—even a sergeant, even an inspector. But that almost never happens. I watch the little children get on and off the school bus to Gerrinsford. At night I check along Trail Street to make sure that shopkeepers have their doors locked. It's been some months since any true emergency rose here."

"Tell me one thing," said Thunstone. "Is there anything unusual in Claines? I mean, a hint of something supernatural?"

Dymock took a sip from the mug. "You've been talking to Mr. Gates, the curate, haven't you, sir? Well, if you look for it, you may find it, then. Some people here do have interesting beliefs. You're staying at Mrs. Fothergill's, as I think. Well, Mrs. Fothergill has a young girl to help her out there, and—"

He stopped a moment. Then: "But perhaps I shouldn't speak of that."

"I wish you would," said Thunstone earnestly. "The supernatural happens to be a chief study of mine."

"Well, someone else is bound to tell you; it's a known thing. That girl's name is Constance Bailey, and she calls herself a witch."

"But witchcraft's no longer a crime in England," Thunstone pointed out.

"No more it is. There are witch groups all over, very public about themselves. Some of them call themselves churches. Constance Bailey makes a point of being a white witch, using sorcery for good."

"And is there anything else out of the ordinary?"

"Only talk here and there. Some do think there are shadowy shapes on the move after dark, just at this time of the year. I haven't taken any such talk seriously."

"Naturally not." Thunstone shook hands with Dymock. "It's been interesting to hear about this. I think I'll go and hunt up some dinner."

"And it's been interesting to hear what you say, too," said Dymock.

Thunstone went back across Trail Street. It was well past five o'clock. He had been in Claines for less than three hours, and he felt a sense of mystery there. Mystery was an active preoccupation with Thunstone.

Swinging his cane, he strolled back along the line of shops. At the fish-and-chips stand, someone came out with a package rolled in newspaper and someone else went in, probably to buy another package. He stopped at the post office to buy stamps, then went to the Moonraven and entered.

Customers lined the bar and several sat at tables. Thunstone went to the bar for a pint of bitter, carried it to an empty table. He brought out his notebook and studied it. Pen in hand, he underscored words and phrases in what he had written, and added the name of Constance Bailey he had heard from Dymock.

# CHAPTER 3

"Yes, sir?" It was a chubby, brown-haired girl in a red and yellow apron, smiling beside his table. "Could I bring you something?"

"If it's something to eat," said Thunstone, smiling back. "What's for dinner this evening?"

"Well, the ordinary is a cut off the joint—leg of lamb today. But if you'd prefer, we can do you a chump chop with two veg and a boiled potato."

"Thanks, I'll have the chop."

"Right, sir."

She scurried away on clicking high heels, fetched back a knife and fork and a folded paper napkin, then clicked away again. Thunstone returned to writing in his notebook. Now and then he glanced around the room. Customers here and there looked back at him, the American stranger in town. One, at least, rather glowered. That was black-bearded Porrask, the garageman, as big as Thunstone, heavily built in his crumpled blue shirt. From that first moment along Trail Street, Porrask had seemed not to like Thunstone, and Thunstone wondered why.

The plump girl waited on customers at other tables. People sitting there greeted her genially. Thunstone heard them call her Rosie. She called them by their first names, too. At last she came to Thunstone again, bearing a plate with meat and vegetables and another with bread and butter. He thanked her and paid for the food. She smiled when he gave her a florin for herself. He began to eat the savory chop, a thick one cut off the loin. He felt hungry enough to relish everything, even some rather watery peas. Rosie came yet again to ask if he would have a dessert. He declined with thanks and sipped at what was left of his pint of bitter.

Someone else came and stopped beside his table. Not the waitress; this time a young woman, not much more than a girl, with a round face and a pointed chin. Her hair, as softly black as soot, hung in banners to either shoulder of the green dress she wore.

She sat down opposite him before he could rise. "Mr. Thunstone, I want to talk to you," she said, in a murmuring whisper. "Would you give me a drink?"

"Of course," he said. "What will you have?"

"Might I have a pink gin?"

He went to the bar and ordered the pink gin and brought it back to the table, then sat in his own chair. She took a sip. The glass trembled in her hand.

"My name's Constance Bailey," she said in her whispering way. "I help at Mrs. Fothergill's. I was there and heard you talking to her, and I watched you go out."

"I knew that somebody watched; I could feel that," Thunstone said. "And I've heard your name. I've heard that you call yourself a white witch."

She widened her eyes when he said that. They were eyes of flecked green. Her lips parted as if to speak, then closed, then opened again.

"Oh," she said at last.

"A white witch is supposed to use her spells for good," said Thunstone, and took another sip of bitter.

Across the floor, Porrask watched from his table and scowled. His hairy hand clamped his beer mug.

"I do try to use my spells for good," said Constance Bailey. "I've cured poor sick children; I've charmed a pest away from gardens. I've told fortunes when somebody wanted a fortune told, and didn't ask for pay. But you make me realize I'm talked about in Claines. And you're talked about in Claines, too, Mr. Thunstone."

"Well," he said, "I suppose a stranger is a rarity."

"You're the sort of stranger who's noticed by people. They wonder about someone like you. Mrs. Fothergill has told some of the neighbors about you, said you're curious about traditions here."

"Which is the truth," said Thunstone. "Will you help me about traditions?"

"Should I?" she asked, her glass at her lips again. "Mr. Thunstone, there are shadows in Claines, and some people realize the shadows are here. Claines is only a small place, but it's so old that nobody knows how it began."

"Mr. Gates said something like that, Mr. Gates, the curate. And so did Constable Dymock."

"You've been questioning people, finding out things. That can cause talk, can't it then? And the questions you ask—perhaps you're sensitive? Psychic?"

"I wouldn't want to claim that," said Thunstone. "That's a special sense that has to be developed. I do observe things and try to puzzle them out."

"Well," she said, "I'm psychic, right enough. I was psychic when I was a little girl, when I was getting my basic training, if you care to call it that, in my white witchcraft. I'm able to see and feel that Claines is haunted."

"Haunted?" Thunstone repeated.

"Please, sir, not so loud. You'd not want to include these other people in what we're saying. Yes, haunted. I look out nights, here and there. And this time of year, there's shadows close at hand. Sometimes I see them in the dark."

She shuddered.

"Ghosts of the dead, you think?" he asked.

"And how long dead, it's not for me to say. Maybe all the way back to the beginnings here, whenever those were. Thousands of years ago."

"I'd like to be with you after dark and see if I could sense them, too," he said.

"No," she said, and took a swallow of pink gin. "Be careful, sir. Especially now, this time of the moon."

"I'm always careful if I can manage," and again he smiled to reassure her. "Not always clever, but always careful. But what about this time of the moon? I've heard about this time of year, but what about the moon?"

"It's like this," said Constance Bailey, drawing out her words. "The moon's on the wax now. It'll be full a week from now. And as it grows in the sky, the shadows are easier to see. Maybe the moon brings them. And then, there are folks here and there in Claines who come on to act strange like when the moon's full."

"There are folks all over the world who act strange at that time," said Thunstone.

She had finished her drink. "I've been trying to warn you," she said, "and I don't seem to be doing a good job of it."

"I've been interested in everything you say, and I thank you."

She rose, and he rose with her. She walked away to the outer door. Porrask scowled after her, then turned back to scowl at Thunstone. When Constance Bailey had gone out, Porrask rose heavily, with a hunch of his big shoulders. He clumped toward Thunstone, carrying his mug. Reaching the table, he stared down. His lips looked loose and ill-humored in his beard.

"Your name's Thunstone, they tell me," he growled.

"Yes, it is."

"Mind if I sit down here a moment?"

"Please do."

Porrask took the chair where Constance Bailey had sat. He put down his mug and crossed his arms on the table. It was a gesture that big men know, to make themselves look bigger.

"My name's Porrask," he said. "Albert Porrask."

"I saw your name on your garage," nodded Thunstone.

"You mean to be in these parts for long?"

"For several days, at least," Thunstone replied. "I'm studying Claines, in a way."

"Ahr," grunted Porrask. He stared into his mug. "I want another of these. Can I bring you one?"

"No, I thank you," said Thunstone, looking into his own pint pot. "I have enough here."

For just then, he had no wish for any favors from this big, resentful garageman.

Porrask got up and stamped to the bar. All his movements were of a bear like heaviness. He brought back his filled mug, sat down again, and drank noisily. "I'm a plain man, Mr. Thunstone," he said, "and I'll just ask you a plain question. Wot is it you're up to in Claines?"

"A plain question," agreed Thunstone, "and I'll give you a plain answer. What I'm doing here comes under the head of my business."

Porrask blinked, but refused to be snubbed. "People do say you ask about Old Thunder and the Dream Rock. And you've been at the curate and Constable Dymock about them."

"News about me seems to travel fast in these parts," said Thunstone. "Maybe I ought to feel flattered."

"Ow," said Porrask, "ain't much as goes on here but wot I hear word of it. And then, you're smarming up to Connie Bailey."

"I talked to her about Claines," said Thunstone evenly. "She came to my table to talk, just as you did."

"Talk about wot?"

"That also comes under the head of my business."

Porrask blinked again. "Look 'ere, sir, you ain't being friendly like, but I'll speak as a friend. Connie Bailey's a witch girl."

"Is she, now?"

"Likely you don't believe in witchcraft."

"Yes, I do."

"Well then, Connie Bailey's a witch. And they used to hang witches, they used. Or burnt them or drowned them."

"Those old laws have been repealed," Thunstone reminded. "Witches can practice their arts today, if they don't break some other law. Anyway, I hear that Constance Bailey is a white witch, does no harm."

Porrask grimaced so fiercely that his beard crawled on his face. He drank a great gulp of beer.

"Just let me tell you a home truth, Mr. Thunstone. If you've come to pry into things about Claines, you'd best go have some talk with Mr. Gram Ensley."

"I've heard the name," said Thunstone. "I believe he owns the big house called Chimney Pots."

"He owns not only that 'ouse but near all the 'ouses in Claines," said Porrask. "Likewise land hereabouts, a good bit of that, all directions. He's rich, is Mr. Ensley, spite of the 'eavy taxes, 'eavy expenses.

Why, he's even got servants. You've got to respect such a man as that."

Thunstone wondered to himself why such a man must be respected. "And what else about Mr. Ensley, beyond the money and property he has?"

"Ow," said Porrask, "he's got brains, too. Knows things as goes on 'ere. Likely by now, he's 'ad word of you. My advice is, go 'ave some talk with him."

"That sounds like good advice," said Thunstone. "I'll try to follow it. To meet him."

"Yus," said Porrask. He swigged down the remainder of his beer, got powerfully to his feet, and tramped away.

Thunstone, too, sipped the last of his own drink, picked up his cane, and went out at the door.

A bus had stopped. People got out and moved away purposefully, bound here or there for the homes that waited for them after the day's work somewhere else. He lifted his wrist and looked at his watch. Half past six, but the sun still up there. Evenings lasted late in England this time of year. He would have time this evening to explore something of Claines.

Carefully he threaded his way through the traffic on Trail Street and on the far side he turned to his left and walked east in front of the small, neatly kept cottages with flowers in the frontyards. Beyond these rose huge, dark-stoned Chimney Pots, with a side street running between its grounds and those of the nearest cottage. That side street ran southward toward the great rise of ground they called Sweepside. Thunstone walked that way, swinging his cane.

The street was gravel-strewn, not paved, with deep ruts. The path on which he walked beside it was set with flat stones like cobbles. He strolled to another graveled street beyond, crossed that, and passed more cottages. A dog came and trotted with him, then abruptly ran into an alley. From afar off came the voices of children, seemingly at play, but he saw no human being.

He passed still more cottages. They looked shabbier than the ones on Trail Street. They were old, subdued in color. One was of crumbling brown brick, another of stone cut long ago. A tawny cat was seated on the thatched roof of that one, looking down at Thunstone with the intent appraisal of cats. The next cottage seemed to have no visible foundation. It might have been washed up on a beach. Thunstone studied the houses. How old were they? Of what century? Claines was old, old.

Overhead swooped a bird, lean and dark, seeming to glide on its unmoving wings. He did not know what bird it was. As it skimmed above him, it emitted a grating caw of sound.

Now he had come to what must be the edge of Claines. The dwellings here looked primitive, almost. He wondered what sort of people lived in them. Nobody was visible, in the yards or at the doors or windows. Yet, he told himself, there must be something inside some of the houses. Perhaps the something, the somethings, watched him.

Before him, between the houses and the coarse grass of the slope, ran a wire fence, breast high. A wooden sign was hung to it:

PRIVATE PROPERTY
DO NOT ENTER
WITHOUT PERMISSION OF
G. ENSLEY

Just the other side of the fence ran a nimble stream of water, a brook perhaps four feet across. It sang happily and scuttled away eastward somewhere. He could not see where it began on Sweepside.

He stepped close against the fence and gazed up the spacious rise of Sweepside to where sprawled the great, uncouth image of Old Thunder.

The white blotch of the figure lay somewhat on a slant. Two men did something at the edge of the thing, perhaps cutting away the turf from the chalk as Gates, the curate, had said. They were dwarfed by Old Thunder. Old Thunder had a round pale blank of a head. This was set without benefit of neck on an awkward-looking oblong body, and below the body extended two thin, unjointed legs that terminated in big flat feet. Primitive, thought Thunstone. Naturally it would be primitive, since its origin must go back to the most primitive of men, or so Gates believed.

Thunstone let his eyes roam over the great green slope. He saw there, singly or in huddles, woolly sheep that cropped at the grass. Two spotted dogs lay at strategic points. Plainly they were there to supervise the flock, guard and govern it.

Sheep, mused Thunstone. Old, old companions of man. Dogs may have been the first animals to join the ancient primitive stone-chippers, but sheep were ancient in the relationship. Some scholars thought they had been tamed as long ago as eight thousand years. Thunstone wondered if the original tamers might not have been children, lugging the little toddling wild lambs home to play with. Wasn't Abel, second son of Adam, called a keeper of sheep in the Book of Genesis? And there was a religious symbolism, too; "The Lord is my shepherd," said the best known of the Psalms. And here on Sweepside above Claines, sheep still were kept and companioned by man as in the long ago, the so long ago.

He turned and looked back along the way he had come.

On the footpath in front of the row of houses toward Trail Street, at a point two crossings back from the fence, stood a motionless figure. It looked as black as a silhouette in ink. It seemed to be dressed in a square, sooty-dark coat despite the warm weather, and drawn low on its head was a broad, slouched hat of the same color. Thunstone started to walk toward it.

At once the figure swiveled around and headed back toward Trail Street. It moved fast, faster than Thunstone. He quickened his own pace. The sooty figure was almost scurrying now. It cut across the street, toward where trees grew in a clump behind Chimney Pots. It vanished among those trees like a shadow.

Thunstone took his own way back to Mrs. Fothergill's. Beside the steps stood a squat black motorcycle, chained to immobility. Another guest had come, then. As he entered the hall, Mrs. Fothergill's ringing voice hailed him from her front room.

"Oh, Mr. Thunstone. A note was left for you."

She came and gave him an unsealed envelope. "Thank you," he said, and opened it.

A small card inside, with smooth script upon it:

Mr. Gram Ensley would esteem it as a favor if Mr. Thunstone would call at Chimney Pots at any convenient time tomorrow morning.

Mrs. Fothergill waited expectantly. "Good news, I hope?" she said. "It's from somebody who wants to talk to me," he said, and mounted the steps to his own room.

He filled a straight-stemmed pipe from a leather pouch, tamped the tobacco carefully, and struck a match to light it. Then he sat down at the little desk. Swiftly he wrote two letters, one to Professor Leslie Spayte at the University of London, the other to Judge Pursuivant in America. Then he searched out his notebook and began to write down yet more of his observations. On one page he set down a list of names:

ELWAIN HAWES, landlord of the Moonraven, a pleasant public house. Food is good there. Hawes is friendly, ditto Mrs. Hawes. They may have information.

DAVID GATES, the curate who presides at St. Jude's. Oxford graduate, young, athletic and proud of it, somewhat intense. Ambitious to be a vicar. Studies the history and prehistory of Claines, wants to write about it, will talk of it.

———— DYMOCK, the local constable, only officer of the law in Claines. Also young, also a university man (Reading), also ambitious. Seems the sort to rise in his profession. Talks readily, though officially. Must talk to him again.

MRS. ALMA FOTHERGILL, my landlady. Cordial, a trifle gushing. Somewhere in her forties, very ready to tell that once she was on the stage. May or may not know a lot about Claines, though she says she was born here.

CONSTANCE BAILEY, who works for Mrs. Fothergill. A rather good-looking girl, black hair, green eyes. Calls herself a white witch. Seems to have something to tell, and seems afraid to tell it. Suggests that Claines has secrets. Must try to find what she's holding back, and why.

ALBERT PORRASK, who operates a garage and machine shop. Big, rough-mannered, truculent. Seems to resent my presence here. Would like to be thought dangerous. Is he? He and others mentioned the name of

GRAM ENSLEY, who owns the biggest house in Claines, and apparently much of Claines besides. Who and what is he?

Thunstone stopped writing and read through all his notes. Then he added a last few words:

Who followed me as I walked through Claines to Sweepside Ridge, and why did he run away?

He closed the notebook and slid it back into his jacket pocket. It had grown dark outside while he had written. He felt tired, though it was not really late as yet. After all, he had been busy in London before he had taken the bus to Claines and had busied himself here.

He stripped off his clothes, hung them up, and from his big suitcase took a light robe and put it on. In the bathroom at the end of the hall he scrubbed his teeth industriously, then turned on a hot shower and soaped his brawny body well from head to foot and rinsed off the suds. Back in his room, he freed the silver blade from his cane and carefully wiped it with a silk handkerchief and sheathed it again. After that, he filled his pipe out of a different pouch from the one he had left in the pocket of his jacket. Without lighting it, he sat to look out at the window.

A wind blew outside, for the ivy-cloaked tree at the side of the house seemed to hunch and weave, seemed almost to walk. The sky overhead was black velvet, spangled all over with winking stars. In one quarter of it stood the moon, pallidly yellow, greatening lopsidedly from its first quarter a few nights ago.

Thunstone sniffed at the bowl of his pipe. It had a special odor, for the tobacco he had stuffed into it was blended with kinnikinnick and the crumbled bark of the red willow. Long Spear, an Indian friend, had told him that to smoke that mixture was a strong guard against all evil magic. He turned toward the window again.

There was no window, only a blurred dimness. And no wall. In just that instant, it was as if Thunstone were somewhere in the open. He strained his eyes to see.

No window, no room. He did not sit in a chair, he perched on a sort of hummock of earth. He moved a foot. Under it turned something like a pebble. He was not in the room he had rented, not anymore. He did not know where he was.

And no moon, no stars. Perhaps no sky. He gathered a sense of a stretch of land, tufted here and there with trees and brush. There was no Trail Street over there, certainly no lights. Far in the distance he sensed, rather than saw, deeply dark hills. Among the tufts moved things, stealthy things, darker than the dimness around them, things perhaps as large as men. They seemed to approach.

Thunstone jammed his pipe into his mouth, rummaged a pack of matches. He struck one alight, and in its glow he saw his room again —the bureau, the door, the bed. He set the flame to his pipe and it glowed redly. He blew puffs of smoke, to the north, the west, the south, the east, then upward and downward. Six puffs in all, as Long Spear had taught him, to the four winds and the two directions, the ancient Dakotah way.

Softly he sang a few words of a song Long Spear had taught him, a song that went back to the Ghost Dance days of Long Spear's people:

*Wahkondah dei dou, wah-pah-din ah tonhie . . .*

A song that prayed for help, that asked Those Above for strength and courage.

Abruptly, he lost all awareness of the tufted plain, the figures skulking upon it, the far dark hills. His room was all around him again, and it was a chair he sat on. He found the light above the bed, switched it on. The bed was there, with comfortable plump pillows and a turned back coverlet.

Thunstone went to the desk and, still smoking, wrote down all that he had seemed to experience. By the time he had finished, the pipe had burned out. He laid it on top of his writing, turned out the light again, and went back to the window. That window remained, sill and sash.

He gazed outward and saw the lights on Trail Street, the glow from the Moonraven across there. He looked up at the sky, at the stars in their courses, their paths and patterns that had been there since the beginning of the time that mankind knew. Cancer, the Crab, soared high above. He remembered things he had heard astrologers say about how the stars ruled life and history, and wondered for the hundredth time if the astrologers truly believed the things they said.

At last he sought the bed he had rented in this old house. It was a comfortable bed, wide enough and long enough for his big frame. He lay with his hands clasped under his head and mused as he lay and, musing, drifted into slumber.

# CHAPTER 4

But Thunstone dreamed. His dreams were confused at first, blurred glimpses of places he had been, people he had talked to in the past. Once he thought he was with a rosy, fair-haired woman known in her circle as the Countess of Monteseco though she had been born Sharon Hill at home in Pennsylvania. She smiled on him, the smile he knew well, and the voice in the dream was her voice. Then she faded into a dark dreamlessness and, without waking, he missed her but was happy to have seen her.

At last came a clear vision. He walked on the sharp, grassy slope of Sweepside, up toward the traced outline of Old Thunder. As he approached, Old Thunder rose suddenly, a powerful, clumsy surge of movement, and loomed over him. The crude outline of the face lived. Its eyes stared down with a concentrated menace. At that Thunstone awoke, to find the sun streaming in at his window.

His watch told him that it was half-past seven. He smiled as he remembered his boyhood, and what his grandmother had said once; that to wake from a dream is always good, because if it was a good dream you were happy to have had it and if it was a bad dream you were glad it was not true. Well, he had had a good dream and a bad dream, and his grandmother had been right about their respective impacts.

He dressed quickly, went to the bathroom to shave and wash, then came back to his own room. There he put his notebook into his pocket and took his cane. He went downstairs and into Mrs. Fothergill's parlor.

"We serve breakfast in here, Mr. Thunstone," she said from the arched doorway to the room behind. "And we have another guest today. But coffee's ready now; would you take a cup?"

"With great pleasure," he said, and went with her to where a dining room was furnished with a cloth-covered table and silver and dishes upon it and chairs set around. Mrs. Fothergill wore a green dress this morning, with white edging at neck and sleeves. They sat down while she filled two cups from a china pot. "Cream in the jug," she said, "and sugar in the bowl."

"I'll just take it black, if you please."

Thunstone drank. The coffee was strong and good. He remembered friends who insisted that good coffee couldn't be had in England. That was like so many sweeping statements, an example to you to avoid sweeping statements on your own part.

"I dare hope," said Mrs. Fothergill, poising her own cup daintily, "that you're finding what you hoped here in Claines."

"I came here with no sure notion of what to find," Thunstone told her, "but I've found out several interesting things." He looked across the table at her. "I'm to see Mr. Ensley today, and maybe he'll be helpful."

"Oh, ah," said Mrs. Fothergill, "I doubt not but that he will."

"I hear that he owns most of the houses in Claines."

"A good lot of them," she said, "but not this one. It so happens that it's been in my family for generations. Mr. Ensley likes to keep an old-fashioned atmosphere in Claines, old-world as you might say. And I don't mind that, I'm sure, though sometimes I miss dear London."

A clatter of feet in the parlor, and a young man entered the room. His long, lank hair and long, lank mustache were more or less the color of strong tea. His jeans pants were tucked into shiny boots. At the open throat of his blue shirt dangled a silver medallion on a chain, with an image Thunstone could not make out. In one hand he carried a massive white helmet.

"Good morning," Mrs. Fothergill greeted him. "Will you have coffee?"

"Yes'm, I thank ye." He laced his cupful with cream and put in several spoonfuls of sugar. He looked at Thunstone. "You passing through, too?"

"Staying for a few days."

"Me, I'm headed down to the coast. Biking there."

Constance Bailey came in from the kitchen. She wore a white apron and a white cap and carried a broad tray. She put down plates for them, each with a lightly fried egg on a slice of toast, two rashers of bacon, and half of a grilled tomato. She set down a toast rack and a jar of marmalade and a butter dish, and went back to the kitchen.

Thunstone found the bacon streaky but somewhat limp, and the tomato rich, red, and savory. After finishing his egg, he took another slice of toast and spread it with butter and marmalade. Mrs. Fothergill poured him more coffee. He was hungry enough to eat everything with relish.

The motorcyclist, too, ate with good appetite, and finished first. He rose and wiped his mouth with his napkin.

"Everything here capital, ma'am," he said to Mrs. Fothergill. "I'll mention your B-and-B to my friends."

"Thank you, that will be good of you," she smiled.

"Not at all."

He went out. They heard the front door slam resoundingly, and a moment later came the fierce rattle of his motor as it started. It went moaning away.

"Well, now," said Mrs. Fothergill, "that was a civil-spoken young man, at least. Some who stop here are, well, matter-of-fact. We still have coffee in the pot, Mr. Thunstone."

"No thank you, don't bother. I'll just finish what I have."

"I've noticed that stick you carry," she said. "It's a very handsome one. Though you don't appear to need it, no lameness if I may say so."

"It was given me by a good friend, and I carry it more or less because he gave it to me," said Thunstone. He pushed back his chair. "I'll be going out now, and of course I'll stay tonight again. I've paid until then, as I remember. Maybe I'll stay on a few days beyond."

"And you'll be welcome, I'm sure."

He went out into the pleasant morning sunshine. Trucks rumbled on Trail Street, and he had to wait for his chance to cross. On the far side, he went into the post office to mail his letters. As he came out, an elderly man passed and nodded in friendly fashion. A pair of girls chattered as they walked along the way. They were dressed almost alike, in slacks and blouses and sandals; but, he could not help noticing, one seemed trim in her simple clothes, the other untidy.

"Good morning, Mr. Thunstone," said Constable Dymock, wheeling his bicycle with him, smiling in the sweep of his mustache.

"Oh, hello there," said Thunstone, as to an old friend. "What a fine day this is, and I've been exploring your little village." He smiled. "Your hamlet, some want to call it."

"And the people of Claines have been exploring you, the best they can manage," said Dymock. "This morning, I've had several come and ask of me, who's that big Yank staying at Mrs. Fothergill's, and what does he want here?"

"Yank," repeated Thunstone. "I can't truly claim that. A Yank lives in the Northern states, and my family is Southern. I was born and raised in the South, and I've lived in the North, so I know the average all around."

"You more or less quote Mark Twain," observed Dymock. "Colonel Sherburn says something like that in *Huckleberry Finn*. Surprised, are you, Mr. Thunstone? But I have been to school, and I always liked American literature."

"I like it, too. And I also like Claines, so far. Interesting, but quiet. The people seem quiet, mostly."

"Here, as elsewhere, the mass of men lead lives of quiet desperation," said Dymock.

Thunstone laughed, because he felt he must. "Quoting American literature again. That's Thoreau, the very first chapter of *Walden*. Is there really that much quiet desperation in Claines?"

Dymock frowned over that. "About the desperation I can't be too sure, but the quietness is here. There's a quiet about it that sometimes seems interesting. Even baleful."

"Why?" asked Thunstone.

"It may be the time of year. Close to the annual turning of the Dream Rock."

"One of the reasons I came here was to watch that annual turning," Thunstone said.

"I'll be watching it, too. Police duty."

Dymock's voice was stern to say that. Thunstone tried to ease his mood.

"It's natural for you to speak like that," he said. "It's characteristic. I find the Englishman to be him of all men who stands firmest in his shoes."

Dymock looked up at that, and a smile relaxed his face. "This time you're quoting Ralph Waldo Emerson. We seem to stick to the American authors this morning, don't we? But I meant to say, Mr. Gram Ensley was out on his front lawn just now, and remarked that he hoped to have you call on him this morning."

"I mean to call, pretty soon. But, Constable, I wonder how I ought to feel about people asking about me here."

"Why, as to that," said Dymock, "part of it may be that you're so big, if I may notice that. An upstanding figure of a man. Maybe the biggest man here just now, except for Albert Porrask."

"Porrask," Thunstone said the name after him. "What should I expect of Porrask? I talked to him last night, at the Moonraven. I didn't know if he was being friendly or not."

"If you had any doubt of that," said Dymock, "you'd better keep that doubt. Maybe he takes notice of how big you are, too. For a long time here, he's been used to people being more or less afraid of him."

"I'm not afraid of him," said Thunstone.

"Good. Well said. But now I must be getting along."

Dymock got on his bicycle and pedaled it away. Watching him, Thunstone saw that he stopped and dismounted again. He was talking to Constance Bailey, who wore brown slacks and a brown blouse, and tossed her dark hair back as she smiled and said something. Dymock smiled, too, not so officially. Thunstone said to himself that they made a nice-looking couple as they stood there together. He walked along toward the church of St. Jude's.

Jude, he pondered. He remembered the General Epistle of Jude. That was one of the shortest books in either Testament, and by no means the most comforting. It was particularly emphatic in its preachment against "murderers, complainers, walking after their own lusts." As for Jude, the author of that Gospel, was he clearly recognized as a saint? He seemed as obscure as the Jude of whom Thomas Hardy had written; he seemed not quite identifiable. Yet the church, and now Thunstone approached it, had been called St. Jude's. For what reason, and for how good a reason?

He came to the edge of the churchyard, to where the Dream Rock lay. He studied it carefully, more carefully than when he had seen it before, with the curate David Gates beside him and talking. Plainly the stone pillar had been meant to suggest a human figure, and upon its head were faint, worn lines that might once have been a face with eyes and a mouth. He touched it with the ferrule of his cane, and as before he felt a humming sensation in his hand and arm.

After a moment, he turned the crooked handle of the cane around and freed the silver blade. He extended the point and touched the Dream Rock with it.

The blade sang audibly, shimmered. He felt the tingling shock so strongly that he fairly snatched his blade away. Some force was in that stone, and whatever it was strove hard against him. He returned the silver weapon to its cane, and bent to lay his hand flat against the fallen pillar.

No sensation this time. Apparently the Dream Rock responded only to the silver that St. Dunstan had wrought. Thunstone turned away and went back along Trail Street.

He looked across to Chimney Pots. Two men were in the frontyard near a white-flowered bush, apparently in conversation. Thunstone crossed over and entered the yard along a pathway of moss-tufted gravel.

The two men looked at him. One was squat and elderly and roughly dressed, and poised a hoe in his hand. The other was taller and almost gracefully slender, and wore a tailored jacket of small black and white checks and gray slacks. As Thunstone came nearer, he saw that this man was smooth-shaven, long-nosed, with creamy gray hair.

He moved with confident steps to meet Thunstone and looked at him searchingly, with eyes that were as dull blue as lead.

"Mr. Thunstone, as I think," he said evenly. "My name is Gram Ensley. So you got my note, did you? So glad you came."

"I got it, and thank you for inviting me."

"Carry on here, Hob," said Ensley to the squat man. "I'll see Mr. Thunstone to the house."

"Yes, sir, right you are," croaked the other man, and put his hoe to the ground. Thunstone followed Ensley to the porch.

That porch was high, made of rough, clinkery stone like the rest of the house. Its pillars rose to a high canopy of fitted slabs two stories above, and the porch floor was faced with rosy-looking old bricks. Ensley led Thunstone up three wide steps and pushed open a massive door of black-painted planks to usher him into a gloomy hallway, paneled in dark wood. Against a broad staircase that mounted upward stood a clothes tree hung with wraps and umbrellas, and next to that a suit of plate armor. Beyond in the house, a piano sounded. Someone was playing Schubert's "Moment Musicale," melodiously but off-hand, as though it were more or less a memory of the music itself.

Thunstone stopped in front of the suit of armor, which stood like a steel image, masked with its visor. It was a fine specimen, delicately patterned here and there. He judged it to be of the early fifteenth century. Against it leaned a great hammer like weapon, with a rusty steel haft some forty inches long. He leaned his cane against the thigh piece of the armor and studied again.

"How beautiful," he said.

As he spoke, the music farther into the house came to an abrupt stop.

"I fear I can't properly identify that armor," said Ensley. "It must have been bought by some Ensley in the past, and set up here. As you see, it was made for a fairly upstanding man, one even of your size, but I wonder if the mace—the hammer there—belongs with the suit. That's a gigantic weight to wield. Hard to pick it up, even with both hands."

"May I try?"

"Of course."

Thunstone stepped closer, put out his big right hand, and lifted the hammer. It was heavy, he knew at once, heavier than sledges used to spike down rails on ties. He studied it a moment, then muscled it out until his arm was straight and horizontal. He could do that. Ensley made a silent gesture as though clapping his hands.

"You'd have been a famous man-at-arms a few hundred years ago," he said.

Smiling, Thunstone leaned the heavy hammer back against the steel figure. Ensley led him to a great side door, opened it, and ushered Thunstone into a spacious room with dark, rich furniture. One wall of the room was shelved, with books on the shelves all the way up to the ceiling. The other walls were hung with drapes of rough, tawny cloth, and upon these were paintings in frames. They were curious paintings, cloudy-looking. A grand piano stood in the center of the floor, but nobody sat at it.

"Who was playing as we came in?" inquired Thunstone.

"Someone I have staying with me here," was the reply. "Won't you sit down?"

Ensley gestured him to a leather-cushioned armchair. "Cigarette?" Ensley offered a silver box with cigarettes so dark as to look almost black. Thunstone could not tell their make.

"Thanks," said Thunstone. "If you don't mind, I'll stick to an old friend I brought along," and he produced his pipe and pouch.

"Of course."

Ensley took a cigarette and sat in another chair. Thunstone filled his pipe and struck a match to it.

"Now then, Mr. Thunstone," said Ensley, "I'll admit to a certain curiosity about you, a curiosity which, by the way, seems to be felt by others in Claines. That's why I asked you to call. What brings you here, may I ask? And how may I help you, if it's help you need?"

He asked the question so winningly, so hospitably, that Thunstone wondered if there were any sincerity in it. He drew on his pipe and smiled.

"Call it curiosity," he said. "I came to England to speak at a meeting and to study in libraries, visit a few sites of old remains. Some friends spoke of this village of Claines, told about the figure of Old Thunder on the slope out there, and of the Dream Rock. They also mentioned some difficulty about getting permission to research such things. So, as I say, I came here from curiosity."

"Curiosity," Ensley repeated him. "I take you at your word, Mr. Thunstone. You're from abroad, and so you can't be representing National Trust or the Department of Environment or any of those. If there's been difficulty about researching here—dragging through land that belongs to me, disturbing the people of Claines—perhaps it can be charged to me and to my people before me. I've even had to go to court a couple of times, but so far there haven't been digs or upheavals at Claines."

"I take it you feel justified in that," said Thunstone. "I might feel the same way if this place belonged to me. I hear that you own most of the houses in Claines, and lands beyond."

"Including Sweepside," nodded Ensley. "I inherited the property, yes. But I've been busy on my own part, making researches as I can. I've tried to inform myself on what to look for, and how to look for it. See here."

He reached from where he sat and from an end table took a flat case the size of a big book. It was covered with a rectangle of glass and exhibited, on a bed of cotton, several flint points. He offered it to Thunstone.

"I've found those on my land," he said. "Found them right here in Claines. I have others; when someone comes upon one, I pay him to bring it to me. Look at the workmanship of those stones."

Thunstone knew something of stone artifacts, and immediately recognized these as fine examples. The largest of them was like a knife blade, say five inches long, tapering, finely flaked along one edge. The others were slender and tapered, like willow leaves. So beautifully were they worked that they suggested jewelry. The colors of the flints were various—rosy, slate-gray, tawny. These were magnificent examples of stone-working skill.

Thunstone studied every item of the collection, and handed it back to his host. "Beautiful," he pronounced. "Skillfully done. I wish a friend of mine were here to look. She's Jean Stuart, at National Geographic in Washington; she knows the Stone Age. Some of those smaller points may have been arrowheads; those people may have had bows."

"Very likely," nodded Ensley.

"They could kill game from far off with bows," said Thunstone. "They could kill men, too, if they understood enemies and war."

Ensley chuckled, rather sardonically. "Undoubtedly they understood enemies and war, and waged war on enemies," he said. "War had already been on earth, for many millennia. Do you read Pfeiffer? There's his book on the shelf there, *The Emergence of Man.* Pfeiffer suggests that Neanderthal man invented war, maybe sixty thousand years ago."

"I've read Pfeiffer," said Thunstone. "In that same sentence, as I remember, Pfeiffer says that Neanderthal man seems to have invented religion. He describes Neanderthal burial sites, with traces of the flowers draped over the skeleton that once was a body." His voice grew sad, for the thought always roused his compassion for those long-ago creatures that were striving to be man, to be Homo sapiens.

"War and religion," said Ensley. "They seem to go together; they seem to have gone hand in hand all the way to the present."

"Whoever your flint-chippers were, they were splendid workmen," said Thunstone. "Where did you find these specimens?"

Ensley smiled at that, a strange, tight smile made by clamping his lips wide across his face. "I dug up those points myself, here on my own property."

"Your property in Claines," said Thunstone.

"Specifically, up yonder on Sweepside. That land, this house—all my property in and about Claines—has been in the Ensley family for hundreds of years."

"And you say you want no explorations on it."

"No explorations that will complicate my own," said Ensley. "I've posted Sweepside against trespassers, but I don't forbid everyone. Mr. Gates, our worthy curate at St. Jude's, may go up there if he wishes and if he promises to be circumspect. But he seems to want to interfere with the figure of Old Thunder; he's outspoken against what he calls paganism." Again he smiled tightly at Thunstone. "Who's the true god of the world, anyway? The god you probably worship has his faults and admits them. In the Ten Commandments he calls himself a jealous god—admits to meanness. Somewhere else he says he won't forgive unto the third and fourth generation."

"You'll find that in the Third Commandment," said Thunstone. "The fifth chapter of Deuteronomy, isn't it? Anyway, that was a long, long time ago."

"Not so very long," shrugged Ensley. "I don't know just how long ago Moses is supposed to have brought down his tables of stone from Mount Sinai, but I'd hazard that Old Thunder's figure on Sweepside was first cut out before that."

He spoke as though he knew what he was talking about. Thunstone drew on his pipe.

"I walked through your little town last evening after supper, as far as your fence at the edge of Sweepside," he said. "When I came back, I saw that I'd been followed by someone, who headed away among some trees behind your house here. I wondered who it was."

"Ah, who indeed?" said Ensley. "What did the person look like?"

"He had a draped coat and a low-pulled hat, so it would be hard to say what he looked like. He was square-built and not very tall, something the figure of your man working outside. The one you called Hob."

"Hob Sayle?" said Ensley. "Hob has been with our family for years, with my father before me. His wife cooks for me, and very well."

He rose, and so did Thunstone.

"See here," said Ensley suddenly. "If you'd like to go right now and walk on Sweepside, I'll take you there. And when we come back, will you take lunch with me? I'll speak to Mrs. Sayle, and I'll wager she'll have something worth the eating."

"Thank you, Mr. Ensley," said Thunstone. "You're being very kind."

"Not at all," said Ensley.

# CHAPTER 5

Ensley went through a door into a room beyond. Thunstone heard him talking, and a woman's voice answering. Then Ensley reappeared.

"I've asked Mrs. Sayle to do us a sort of justice at lunch," he said. "She says she has good seafood—this is a Friday—and a salad which she says will be a dream of spring, and some kind of sweet to follow. Does that sound good?"

"It sounds delicious," Thunstone replied.

They went out together, upon the broad porch.

"That stick of yours interests me," remarked Ensley. "Yet, if I may say so, you don't seem to need it to walk with."

"I carry it for old time's sake," said Thunstone. "It was given to me by a valued friend, Judge Keith Hilary Pursuivant."

"I've heard that name," said Ensley, nodding. "An American student of the occult and famous in his chosen field. Rather like yourself, I should think."

"I'm flattered," said Thunstone, "to be thought like Judge Pursuivant in any way whatsoever."

"Are you ready for our little walk?"

They stepped down from the porch and walked around the house to the left. On that side, yew trees grew close to the rough, dark wall, with barred windows looking down upon them from above. A slate-faced path skirted close to the yews. Beyond and behind the house, Ensley led the way to another path, moss-carpeted, that ran between clumps of trees. It was hard to see the houses of Claines from that position.

"We can go directly to a gate this way," said Ensley. "Allow me to wonder, Mr. Thunstone, about your name. It has a legendary sound."

"I can't speak to its origin," said Thunstone. "I do know that the name is English, and that an ancestor of mine came to Virginia in 1642. I haven't found any Thunstones here in England, not that I've looked very carefully."

"According to the old story of Tom Thumb, King Thunstone succeeded King Arthur," said Ensley.

"I didn't know that anyone succeeded King Arthur," said Thunstone. "I thought that when he was carried to Avalon by the three queens, the Saxons took over."

They had come past the trees by now, walking among currant bushes. Sweepside was visible beyond.

"Why, as to that," said Ensley, "Thunstone is a name with a Saxon sound, and there were various Saxon kings after Arthur. Come this way to our gate through the fence."

Together they approached the gate in the wire. It was a simple gate, of weathered wooden slats nailed upright to two horizontal bars. On the far side, a roughly made bridge of stone slabs lay across the little stream. Ensley lifted a heavy hasp, opened the gate, and stepped aside to let Thunstone enter before him. Then he followed and hooked the gate behind them. Far up the slope showed the considerable stretch of Old Thunder, with the two men busy at its edge. Thunstone and Ensley turned their steps in that direction. All along the slope grazed sheep, some of them close at hand. The ground sprouted heavy green grass, with tufts of flowered gorse here and there.

"I've asked about your name, and that gives you the right to wonder about mine," said Ensley. "My given name, I mean, Gram."

"Now that you speak of it, I don't think that I've met with the name of Gram, either," replied Thunstone. "Unless it's a form of Graham."

"No, just Gram. It's always been Gram. A younger son gets the name in my family. You see, we're titled—baronets—and my older brother has the title, and the manor, up north of here. But I was named Gram, and I got Chimney Pots and the estate here."

"It's an interesting old house," Thunstone said. "It must be very old."

"Most parts of it are. Here and there it's been rebuilt over the centuries. Now, here we come to what the people call Old Thunder."

They had come there indeed. Close at hand, the outline showed as a sort of ditch dug in the turf, a ditch fully two feet wide and several inches deep and many feet long on an uneven curve. Pale, chalky soil showed through. Ensley led the way toward where the men dug with flat shovels. One of them straightened up. It was Porrask, broad and bearded, wearing wrinkled work clothes.

"We've been at it since after breakfast, sir," he addressed Ensley. "How does it look?"

"First-rate," replied Ensley. "You've done well here. Others will take your places in an hour or so. Any complications?"

"Well, you might call something a complication," said Porrask. "Look up yonder, sir, where that clump is. That little witch girl, Connie Bailey's there, all hunkered over, up to something."

Ensley wheeled to look. A hundred yards or so up the slope crouched a little figure in brown, its hands busy.

"Why didn't you tell her she was trespassing?" growled Ensley. "Are you still sweet on her?"

"Well—" stammered Porrask embarrassedly.

"Since you didn't tell her, I shall."

Ensley strode away purposefully, and Thunstone walked with him.

As they approached, the figure straightened to its feet. It was Constance Bailey, sure enough. She stood and waited. As they came close, Thunstone saw that her black hair looked tumbled, her eyes were wide with apprehension. She held a little sheaf of green stems with yellow flowers, in hands that trembled.

"See here, my girl, I've had to warn you off my property before this," Ensley said forbiddingly. "I thought I'd put up signs enough to warn anyone who could read. I'll ask you to leave at once."

"I didn't mean any harm, Mr. Ensley," quavered Constance Bailey. "I only came to pick some of this Saint-John's-wort."

She held out her fistful of gathered plants, as though it might plead for her.

"You throw that down," Ensley snapped.

"But please, it's nothing to harm," she begged. "It's a good plant, can help people."

"Throw it down," ordered Ensley, more fiercely.

She sighed, and obeyed. The plants fluttered to the ground from her slim hands.

"Mr. Ensley," she said timidly, "I'm sorry if I did wrong, but could I ask permission to come back—gather—"

"Yes, you did wrong," Ensley broke in. "You've forfeited any right to ask favors from me. Get off this land, then. You're a trespasser here, and you can be thankful that I don't prosecute you. Go on, go away."

"Y-yes, sir."

She went, her head bowed. Ensley watched and said nothing. Thunstone, too, was silent until Constance Bailey reached the fence at the bottom of the slope and went along it to the gate.

"Saint-John's-wort," muttered Ensley. "Black magic."

"I don't believe it's that, not quite," interposed Thunstone. "It's always been used to fight black magic, even against vampires and werewolves, and I've heard that it's good as a medicine."

"Maybe I should have let her pick more of it, at that," said Ensley. "I know it can hurt sheep if they eat too much of it, can make their skins sore."

"Do you mind if I pick up what she threw down?" asked Thunstone.

"Not at all, if you like. You're my guest here, not a trespasser like that little girl pretending to witchcraft."

Thunstone brought out an envelope, knelt and carefully gathered the scattered stems. Flecks of pinkish red showed on the yellow blooms. He stowed them in the envelope, taking care not to bruise or break them, then slid the envelope into his inside pocket.

Constance Bailey had left Sweepside by then, had gone out of their sight. Ensley and Thunstone returned to the figure of Old Thunder. The head of the figure showed immense and pallid with the removal of turf, and two blotchy eyes were visible where greenery had been left. Thunstone looked at the semblance thoughtfully. The face bore a look of the face on the Dream Rock.

"How old might Old Thunder be?" he asked Ensley, who shrugged.

"That's difficult to answer. They've always said that he's always been here."

"Might the Druids have dug him out? The pagan Celts?"

"No," replied Ensley. "Druids were newcomers, hardly in England before the fifth century B.C. As for the Celts, they ruled here before the Romans, but most scholars think they came along from the European mainland, maybe even from what's now Russia. Men were here, flourished here, long before the Celts."

"So far as my study goes, they flourished here for hundreds of thousands of years," said Thunstone. "Piltdown man was a hoax, of course. But there's Swanscombe man, dated a quarter of a million years ago."

"Probably he was our ancestor, yours and mine," nodded Ensley. "England must have been tropical then, between the Ice Ages. Elephants here, and the rhinoceros. And Swanscombe man too, chipping flints and living a good food-gathering life. But I doubt that he made Old Thunder here. I'd judge that Old Thunder is as early as any hillside image we have in England. But, I'd hazard, no more than ten thousand years ago, just yesterday compared to Swanscombe man."

"Ten thousand years!" exclaimed Thunstone, and Ensley laughed.

"It seems long to you, eh? But how long has been the life of mankind? Now then, shall we go back to the house? Lunch will be ready soon."

Thunstone lowered the ferrule of his cane to the bared chalk of Old Thunder's outline. He felt a tingle in his hand and arm, not as strong as the one he had felt when he had investigated the Dream Rock, but it was there. He drew his cane away and went along with Ensley, to the gate at the foot of the slope. They retraced their steps through the currant bushes and around the side of the house.

Inside, Thunstone leaned his cane to the suit of armor that stood in the hall. Ensley escorted him into the book-lined front room.

"A splash of something to drink before lunch?" he urged. "Here, will you have whiskey?"

"Thank you."

Ensley took a bottle from a sideboard and poured into two glasses. Then he spurted soda from a siphon—a gasogene, that was called by Holmes and Watson in the old stories—and handed one to Thunstone. "Cheers," he said, lifting his own drink.

"Cheers," Thunstone echoed him, and sipped. It was scotch, of course. When the English said whiskey, they meant scotch. It was good scotch.

"You say you came here for curiosity's sake," said Ensley. "With someone like you, though, that means research. How does your research come on?"

"I don't know if it's truly research," smiled Thunstone. "I can only say that I'm glad I visited Claines. As for what I'm after, suppose I just call myself a truth seeker."

"Truth seeker," repeated Ensley, and took another swallow of his drink. "A looker into the nature of reality, is that it? Well, perhaps I'm a truth seeker, too. What is truth?"

"Pontius Pilate asked that once, and didn't wait for Jesus to answer him," said Thunstone. "It's a pity he didn't wait; Jesus was apt to give interesting answers to questions. The nature of reality, you say. The demonstrated fact is, when strange things are examined, the strangeness goes out of them. They become workaday facts. The impossible is always happening."

"I like that," said Ensley, wagging his head over it. "You're right, Mr. Thunstone; you have a way of being right. For instance, an impossibility like space travel has become a familiar thing, almost a commonplace. The splitting of the atom—I suggest it's too bad that we made a reality out of that. What else? What story that's called impossible today? The vampire? The werewolf? The dead rising to haunt us?"

Thunstone did not remark that he had in his time encountered vampires, werewolves, and ghosts of the dead, all three. "What you mean," he did say, "is that rationalization can take the super out of supernatural."

"True again," applauded Ensley. "You've finished your drink; will you take another? No? Then let's go into the dining room and see what Mrs. Sayle has for us."

The room behind had a long table of dark, polished wood, set with lacy mats and silver and plates. A woman waited there, pudgy and round-faced, with red-dyed hair. She wore an apron worked in blue yarn with stars. As Ensley came in, she looked at him almost apprehensively. Plainly she feared him.

"This is Mr. Thunstone, Mrs. Sayle, and I hope you've done us justice today," Ensley said loftily.

"Ow," she said, "quite simple, I fear, but I hope good. I'll just fetch it in."

And she bustled out.

Ensley sat at the head of the table, and Thunstone at a place beside him. There were glasses of cold white wine. Mrs. Sayle scurried in again with something in an oval china tureen, and held it for them to help themselves. It turned out to be a creamy Newburg of shrimp, and with it she served them small potatoes and greens cooked with tiny slivers of ham. There was also a salad of lettuce, sauced with something mustardy. Then she brought a straw tray with slices of crusty bread. Nothing simple about this lunch, thought Thunstone as he ate with a good appetite. He wondered why Mrs. Sayle sounded nervous.

"Those greens are picked here and there on my property," Ensley told Thunstone. "Wild greens. Hob gathers them; he knows which are good."

"Delicious," said Thunstone, eating a forkful.

"I take leave to observe how impressed you are with evidences of antiquity in and around Claines," said Ensley, refilling Thunstone's wineglass from a carafe.

"Naturally I am," agreed Thunstone. "In America, we date antiquities back no further than, say, Jamestown and Plymouth Rock. Oh yes, and in Spanish America, to Columbus and the various conquests. Earlier than these things, we're prehistoric. Though we're not young in our prehistory, either. Some paleontologists reckon that men have been in America for forty thousand years, maybe even longer than that."

"Forty thousand years makes my researches here seem only of yesterday," said Ensley. "I mentioned, as I remember, that I incline to date Old Thunder at ten thousand years ago, the late Stone Age. But to that modest yesterday I pay very much attention."

Thunstone was silent for a moment, then decided to say what he had in mind. "I wondered why you were so short and sharp with that pathetic little girl on Sweepside," he said. "Constance Bailey."

Ensley grimaced and glared above his wineglass. "That little poseur, that trickster," he snarled out. "With her pretense of being a witch, what she calls the Old Religion. How old is witchcraft?"

"It's prehistoric, I suppose," said Thunstone.

"It's a newcomer," pronounced Ensley. "There are some oldish things in it, but for the chief part it's just a mockery of various established faiths. Here, and in Europe generally, it's a mockery of Christianity, apes Christianity and rebels against it. Among the Jews, it sneers at the Talmud. It's anti-Koran among Moslem peoples, and so on. And this Bailey wench, she coos her promises to ignorant people in Claines, tricks them into thinking she can help them." He furrowed his face. "Those are some of the things I hold against her. Her witchcraft is parvenu, a lot newer than my yesterday we talked about."

"Does she do harm?" Thunstone asked.

"She's a nuisance. I don't have time for nuisances in Claines."

Thunstone changed the subject. "You feel confident that you can refer the Old Thunder image to times ten thousand years ago."

"Well, as to that, stone tools have been turned up in the chalk of the outline. A couple of those points I showed you came from there. I suggest that Paleolithic people first dug Old Thunder out of the turf and down to the chalk for all to see."

They finished their lunch, and Thunstone reflected that it had been a fine one, that Mrs. Sayle had not needed to apologize for it. Or had she? He and Ensley left the table, and in the front room Ensley chose another decanter from the sideboard and poured them small snifters of brandy. It was excellent brandy.

"I've decided to show you something else I've dug up hereabouts," said Ensley. "Something I don't show everyone."

He pulled open a drawer in a desk and took out what seemed to be a bone, slender and brown with age, and perhaps eight inches long. He handed it to Thunstone. "What do you make of it?" he asked.

"I'd say it came from the wing of a large bird," said Thunstone.

"From the wing of an eagle, I'd hazard. And look at it; it's been worked."

Thunstone turned the bone over and over in his big hands. At the large end appeared a deep notch, and along the length showed six small holes that must have been made by a drill. There were scratched lines here and there, in triangles and squares.

"It seems to have been a flute," said Thunstone, handing it back. "Did men of the Old Stone Age have those?"

"To judge from this one, they did. Probably they made some of their flutes from wood or reeds, long ago gone to dust. And undoubtedly they had drums, too, drums that have perished. But this is of bone. It has survived the thousands of years."

Ensley set the notched end to his pursed lips, arranged his fingertips on the holes. Blowing, he achieved a trill of sound, and the movement of his fingers made it turn into a strange, minor melody. Thunstone felt a current within himself, like the current he had known when he had touched the Dream Rock, the outline of Old Thunder. Ensley lowered the flute and grinned.

"They could make music of a sort, right enough," he said. "What else interests you, Mr. Thunstone?"

"These paintings of yours," said Thunstone.

He took time to study the paintings. Two of them were so blurry as to defy critical appraisal. Another seemed to be a view of Sweepside, complete with Old Thunder, but there was an impression of fog. The last of the display was clear enough. It showed a prone cross with a human figure spiked to it, and around this danced a dozen smaller figures, grotesquely proportioned.

"Who did these?" he asked Ensley.

"My friend who's staying here," Ensley replied, stowing the bone flute back in its drawer. "Talented at painting and other things. But from time to time she turns to me for guidance."

She, Ensley had said. His guest, then, was a woman who could paint, could play the piano. Why hadn't she appeared for lunch? Thunstone did not ask.

The two talked about trifles in Claines, and finally Thunstone took up his cane and said his good byes and thanks.

"Not at all," said Ensley. "I've come to the conclusion that your presence here has its certain importances. Now, let's see; tomorrow is Saturday the third, and I fear I'll be fairly well occupied. What are your plans for Sunday?"

"I've been asked to come to church, and I'll do that."

"Well then, after church, would you care to come here for noon dinner and some more talk?"

"I'd be very glad to come."

He walked out. Hob Sayle, at his work in the frontyard, stared after him but said nothing.

He strolled past the cottages to the west of Chimney Pots and to Mrs. Fothergill's. Entering, he mounted the stairs. In the hall above, Constance Bailey plied a broom.

"Do you ever ride that broom?" he teased her.

"I just sweep with it," she said shyly.

From his pocket he brought the envelope with the Saint-John's-wort.

"Here," he said, "these are the plants Mr. Ensley made you throw away. I picked them up and saved them to give to you."

"Oh!" she half-gasped and reached out for the envelope. Her slender fingers trembled against his thick ones. "Oh," she said again. "I thank you, Mr. Thunstone."

"I didn't think that a plant called Saint-John's-wort could be an evil one." He smiled down at her.

"No, it's good," she said. "Mix its juice with olive oil and wine, and it's good for cuts and bruises. You can rub it in for arthritis. It's a holy plant."

"And, being a white witch, you try to do good."

"Yes, yes, and I know poor people in Claines who can be helped by this. Thank you again."

He went into his room, sat down, and brought out his notebook to write down a number of things that had occurred to him during his visit with Ensley. After that he wrote a letter to Judge Pursuivant in America.

Outside in the hall, Constance Bailey bustled at her work. She began to sing, in a rather tuneful voice. Thunstone knew it was an old song, one he had heard when he was a little boy:

> One I love, two I love,
> Three I love, I say,
> Four I love with all my heart,
> And five I cast away . . .

Listening, Thunstone smiled above the pen in his fingers. For a moment, he almost joined in the song for the sake of old times, but decided against that. He let her sing the next verse by herself:

> Counting leaves is not the way
> A body's love to prove,
> For the very one I cast away
> Is the very one I love.

He heard her move away to work somewhere else. He studied the letter he had written and put it in an envelope. He thought of all he had heard, all he had wondered, since coming to Claines. He mused on a hint, from somewhere, of danger.

Finally he made a careful copy of all his notes from the first, and this took him considerable time. He wrote on a card, in big letters:

SEE IF THIS INTERESTS YOU. IF YOU DON'T HEAR FROM ME BY MONDAY OR TUESDAY, COME TO CLAINES AND SEE WHAT'S HAPPENED. YOU MAY WANT TO BRING HELP.

J. THUNSTONE

He folded the sheaf into the largest envelope he had brought with him and addressed it to Professor Leslie Spayte at the University of London. He put stamps on the bulging envelope, and took both his letters out to seek the post office.

# CHAPTER 6

Thunstone's watch said it was nearly five o'clock. Overhead, dull clouds had begun to roll up across what earlier had been a sky of soft blue. They rose above the horizon to westward and sent out exploratory tendrils of dark gray. Thunstone headed past Albert Porrask's machine shop. Porrask was inside the open door, his massive body stooped as he peered into the motor of an automobile. Next door, at the Waggoner pub, a little knot of men lounged. As on the previous evening, they were waiting for the door to open.

He strode past the side street along which he had adventured to Sweepside, and looked at Old Thunder. On the white border line of the huge, rude image clung two dark dots, men working to cut and smooth away the turf to let the white chalk show through. Porrask and his mate who had been there earlier must have been relieved by another pair, and Ensley had seemed to have something to do with directing the work and its performers. Thunstone remembered how Ensley had spoken praise to Porrask, condescendingly lofty praise, and had told him he would be relieved at the job of outlining the figure. That had been a casual dismissal of sorts for Porrask. Then Ensley had flared into anger when Porrask had called his attention to Constance Bailey at her herb-gathering. Certainly there had been nothing casual about Ensley's dismissal of her. However Ensley supervised the annual repair of Old Thunder, Constance Bailey was to have no part in it. Thunstone had felt embarrassment that he had been present at her banishment.

He passed the cindery-dark pile of Chimney Pots across Trail Street, and again approached the little church they called St. Jude's. Gates, the curate who wanted to be a vicar, likely sat in his study, but

Thunstone had no notion of calling on him there. Gates would certainly be at work on his sermon for day after tomorrow, the sermon he had promised to make memorable in Claines.

Thunstone paused beside the Dream Rock, but this time he did not touch it with the ferrule of his cane. He studied the markings upon it. At what would have been the upper end before the thing fell were the remains of carved or chiseled lines, washed and worn by who could say how many centuries, that might have suggested eyes and mouth, a face that looked up at him. Nor was that face dissimilar to the greater outline of Old Thunder's face on Sweepside yonder. Elsewhere on the fallen pillar showed a faint pattern of marks like chevrons, with lines and loops. Writing of a sort? Did the ancient dwellers at Claines tread the fringe, the threshold of true writing? Thunstone wished for several scholarly friends, men whose judgment would be better than his, to come and study the Dream Rock. They might even manage to decipher the writing, if writing it truly was, might give its message to the modern world.

He continued on his way past the church, past the last house on Trail Street, and reached the murky stream that bounded Claines to the east. He had had a walk of considerably more than a mile. He moved out on the concrete bridge and leaned on the rusted iron railing and looked down into the water.

It moved slowly, did the water of Congdon Mire. It had nothing like the bright ripple of the little brook at the foot of Sweepside, the brook that must flow into it. The current crawled as dark as a shadow in winter. No light bounced upon it from the sky overhead that was now well cloaked with clouds. Congdon Mire rolled stealthily below the bridge, seemed to writhe its way along like a great gloomy snake. There was no way of judging depth, but Thunstone could guess that anyone who fell in would be over his head. He surveyed the flow and wondered at the proportion of solid matter in the liquid. And what sort of solid matter?

As he stared, light came from somewhere into that slow current. First came flashes, as if reflected from a mirror. Then circles like halos, one after another, glowing, blinding, greatening, rising. He had a sense of faintness, and clutched at the upper rod of the iron railing.

Into his ears stole a throb, like a ruffle of approaching drums. He planted his feet apart to hold himself where he was.

"Sir, are you all right?"

It was the voice of Constable Dymock, anxiously raised. Dymock pedaled his bicycle swiftly along the bridge and sprang off to catch Thunstone strongly by the elbow. His mustache quivered. "Are you all right?" he asked again.

"I am, now I am," Thunstone replied. He was not looking into Congdon Mire now, and his head cleared. "I had a feeling of faintness just now; I don't know why."

Dymock still held him by the arm. "Some people do go dizzy here on the bridge," he said. "Once or twice, someone has fallen in. I've had that feeling myself in my time."

"Why does it happen?" asked Thunstone, feeling better.

"I've wondered that, but I've never heard it explained. It seems to affect walkers on the bridge at this time of year, more or less. The weather, I fancy."

"The weather's been beautiful," said Thunstone. "Even if it rains."

Dymock stooped and picked up Thunstone's cane. "Here, you dropped it. Handsome stick, that. Good job it didn't fall off the bridge."

"I'm glad I didn't lose it," said Thunstone, taking the cane back. "It was given to me by an old friend." He turned back toward Claines. "Thanks for troubling about me."

"Not at all."

They walked along the bridge together, Dymock trundling his bicycle. A truck passed them. Its driver honked and waved, and Dymock waved back. "I know that chap," he said. "He delivers dairy products along this highway. I see him sometimes at the Moonraven. He says he wouldn't live in Claines if they gave him free rent."

They were off the bridge now, walking along beside Trail Street. "Why won't he live in Claines?" Thunstone asked.

"As I remember his talk, he was made nervous by Old Thunder up there on the hill. Says he spent one night in Claines—it so happens that it was this time of year again, around the first of July. He stayed at Mrs. Fothergill's where you're staying." Dymock looked thoughtful. "He says that Old Thunder came to his window where you're staying."

"I had a sort of dream of my own there last night, but nothing about Old Thunder," said Thunstone. "All right, Officer, what do you make of all this strange evidence?"

"It's not evidence so far, only conjecture, only a question. The first thing I learned at police school was to stick to facts, not conjectures."

They were passing St. Jude's by now. Both of them glanced down at the Dream Rock. It looked like a long carcass of some sort, a carcass flayed and pallid.

"May I say something, Mr. Thunstone?" said Dymock suddenly. "Connie Bailey said you were kind to her today."

"Oh, that," said Thunstone. "She'd gathered some plants and dropped them, and I picked them up and saved them for her."

"You were kind to her," repeated Dymock.

"You seem to like her," ventured Thunstone.

"Yes, sir, I do like her. I don't know why Connie is hated and mistrusted in some quarters; she never tries to hurt anyone. She does call herself a white witch. But now, I'd suppose that *witch* is a word coming from wit or wisdom, and perhaps she'd be better off to call herself just a wise woman. Because she does have wisdom."

"As I understand, the word *witch* seems to derive from the old Saxon word *wicca,*" said Thunstone. "*Wicca* meant sorcery. *Wickedness* may be a word related to *wicca,* and some argue that."

"In any case, there's nothing wicked about little Connie," said Dymock definitely, "and there's nothing on the statute books to say that witchcraft of itself is a crime. I've no reason to suspect her or arrest her."

They were walking in front of the Waggoner pub. Men moved into it and out of it. "What sort of place is that?" Thunstone asked.

"Oh, quite respectable, I'd call it," replied Dymock. "Yes, and needed here. The Moonraven is a capital place, but Claines is a trifle big for just the one pub. The Waggoner takes care of the overflow from the Moonraven, and it has a clientele of its own." He leaned his bicycle beside the front door. "I'll go in, just for a check. Would you care to join me?"

"Thanks, I'll have some dinner at the Moonraven." Thunstone looked at his watch. "It's a minute or so past six, time to eat."

"I hope to talk with you again," said Dymock, and entered the Waggoner.

As Dymock went in, Porrask came out. He stood with his feet planted wide and watched Thunstone walk along the street. After a moment, he followed.

Thunstone came to the paved space in front of the Moonraven and paused for a moment beside a parked car. Without seeming to, he saw Porrask approaching. He went into the Moonraven and to the bar, where Mrs. Hawes filled him a pint mug of lager. A number of customers sat here and there, eating and drinking. Thunstone carried the mug to a table and hung his cane on the back of a chair. Porrask, too, approached the bar, ordered a drink, and went to another table.

The plump waitress came smiling to where Thunstone sat. "Would you be taking dinner with us, sir?" she asked.

"What's for dinner tonight?"

"Well, it's Friday, and we have good fish, fresh or smoked. Or if you don't fancy fish, maybe a nice slice of ham with peas."

"What's your fresh fish and what's the smoked fish?" Thunstone asked her.

"The fresh is fried plaice and the smoked is finnan haddie. Chips with either one, of course, and a salad."

"Let me have the plaice and chips," decided Thunstone. "As for the salad, can you just bring me some lettuce and some oil and vinegar? I'll mix my own."

"Very good, sir, thank you sir."

She trotted away to the kitchen door. Thunstone took a sip of his lager. People at the bar and at the tables chattered. From a radio set came a reedy, mournful strain of music. Porrask sat drinking. He stared toward Thunstone without looking directly at him.

Some minutes passed, and the waitress fetched a tray to Thunstone and set down a plate of fish and chips, another with a pale green wedge cut from a head of lettuce, and cruets of oil and vinegar. He paid her and tipped her. Carefully he shredded the lettuce in his big fingers, poured on oil, then sprinkled salt and pepper. He stirred the salad with a fork, ate a morsel, approved it, and then tried the fish. It was crisply brown and sweet. He seasoned it with vinegar and dripped some on the chips.

Porrask was eating, too, an enormous sandwich from the edges of which fluttered red fringes of ham. He finished his pint, went to the bar, and brought himself back another. Sitting again, he scowled down at the mug, then scowled toward Thunstone. Other customers chatted over their plates and mugs.

Thunstone finished his dinner and let the waitress clear away the plates. He sipped slowly at his pint of lager. Porrask was heading back for what would be his third.

"Mr. Thunstone," said the subdued voice of Constance Bailey. She stood diffidently beside his table. At once he was on his feet.

"Sit down," he invited. "Could I bring you something? Gin and bitters suits you, I believe."

"Yes, please, if you will."

He sought the bar and paid for the gin and bitters, and fetched the glass to the table. Constance Bailey murmured her thanks and sipped. She looked at him with round, troubled eyes.

"You were kind to me, Mr. Thunstone," she said. "Keeping the Saint-John's-wort for me as you did."

"Not at all. I just happened to think of it."

"The thinking of it was kindness," she insisted. "But, Mr. Thunstone, I came hoping to find you here, to talk to you. Warn you, I might say."

"Warn me?" he repeated.

At that moment, Porrask began to sing, loudly and hoarsely:

> He came home the first night,
>   as drunk as he could be,
> He saw a head upon the bed
>   where his head ought to be.
> "My kind wife, my loving wife,
>   my dear wife," said he,

"Whose head is upon the bed
where my head ought to be?"

The others in the room had stopped talking to listen. A pudgy man with short gray hair snorted with amusement. The woman with him looked shocked.

"You just don't know, Mr. Thunstone," said Constance Bailey in a hurried voice. "Things get out and walk at night, this time of year. You can hear things, see things, around the time they turn the Dream Rock."

"I did have a sense of something outside, last night," said Thunstone. "But you say you want to warn me. Warn me against what?"

"Danger," she replied. "Something's up this turning time, something bad. And you're going to be in it, maybe get hurt. You oughtn't to have come at turning time."

"I came on purpose because I wanted to see the turning," he said. "How do you know I'm in danger?"

"Don't ask me how I know. It's a witch's business to know things, see them before they happen. And you're a kind man, a good man, and I don't want any bad thing to come to you."

She was utterly in earnest. Her eyes were wide; she clenched her glass in her hand.

"Mr. Gram Ensley's up to something, with all his study of those old pagan folk who used to live here," she said. "He raised them from the dead, I think. And with you here, he wants you in it somehow."

"I don't understand that," confessed Thunstone.

"I don't truly understand it myself. But I can see things, I tell you. I'm a white witch—"

"One who does her works for good," supplied Thunstone, smiling, and from the corner of his eye he saw that Porrask didn't like the smile.

"I can see things to come," repeated Constance Bailey, again in a voice barely audible. "When I was just a girl, somebody taught me. I say that this time of year, when they turn the Dream Rock, the nights go strange."

"Yes, you've said that. And I heard it today from someone else. But how do the nights go strange?"

"Maybe I'm the only one who can feel and see," she said. "I don't know anyone else who can. Not Mrs. Fothergill. She tells me not to talk foolishness. And Mr. Gates doesn't believe, either. So I don't talk to anyone about it."

"Talk to me," Thunstone invited her.

"Well," and her hands fluttered, "after dark, at the turning time of year, this place can be different. I can look out the window and see another kind of country, no houses on it, not even the house I'm in myself. And bits of brush, and things moving in them, like a bad dream everywhere, though I'm awake. And nobody believes me."

"I believe you," said Thunstone, "because that's how it was with me last night."

Her eyes grew wider still. "You saw it, you felt it? You've got the second sight in you?"

He shook his head. "I've never thought of myself as being particularly psychic, at least not any more than most people. I do believe that certain sensitivities can be developed. Maybe I've done something like that."

"You saw that other empty dark land too?" she almost cried out. "Now I know you'll come to danger in it."

Porrask sang again at his table, sang with all his might, beating time with his mug:

> "You old fool, you damn fool, you son of a bitch,"
> said she,
> "It only is a cabbage head my mother sent to me."
> "I've traveled on land, I've traveled on sea,
> a thousand miles or more,
> But I never saw a cabbage head with whiskers
> on before."

"That'll be quite enough of that, Mr. Porrask!" called out Hawes from beside the bar.

Everyone in the room had fallen silent, was watching. Porrask paid no attention to Hawes's warning. He surged to his feet, a great rough rock of a man. He stamped resoundingly toward the table where Constance Bailey sat with Thunstone. Stooping, he peered into her face and licked his bearded lips.

"Why don't you get out of here, and proper stay out of here, you little witch girl?" he growled thickly. "I saw Mr. Ensley put you off his property today. He doesn't like witches, and neither do I. You ought to be driven right out of Claines."

"I don't have anything to say to you," stammered Constance Bailey, manifestly frightened.

"Oh, you don't? But I've got something to say to you, then, not 'alf I don't."

"No, you haven't anything to say to her," said Thunstone. He was out of his chair, swiftly and lightly for all his size. "She told you she doesn't want to talk to you. Leave her alone."

Porrask straightened up, hiked his big shoulders, and fixed bright, murderous eyes on Thunstone.

"Gor lumme, it's the sodding Yank we've got 'ere in town," he said. "So you want to take up for little witchy-bitchy here?"

All the other customers watched, in taut, expectant silence.

"You want to know what I think?" mouthed Porrask.

"It doesn't make a bit of difference to me what you think about anything," said Thunstone. "Go away and stop bothering us."

"Why, goddamn you—"

Hawes came hurrying to them. "Come on, Mr. Porrask, you're making a fool of yourself."

"Fool, is it?" roared Porrask. His face was flushed as red as a tomato; his eyes rolled. He pushed Hawes away from him, so violently that Hawes staggered and almost fell. Then he swung around to face Thunstone again.

"How would you like to get knocked on your bum?"

"I wouldn't like it," said Thunstone, "so don't try it."

A concerted gasp went up from the onlookers as Porrask lumbered at Thunstone and threw his big, hairy right fist.

Thunstone bobbed skillfully. The fist went singing past his temple. Instantly he stepped in close, clutching Porrask's meaty upper arms in his broad hands. Porrask strove to shake free, but Thunstone clamped hard, his thumbs questing along the inner lines of the biceps and then driving in hard on the nerves there. Porrask howled in sudden pain. Thunstone expertly kicked his feet out from under him. Porrask floundered heavily down upon the broad planks of the floor.

"You bloody, sodding Yank!"

Porrask rolled over with hands and knees under himself and struggled up again. He clawed at Thunstone with his right hand, its fingers crooked like talons, searching for the face. Thunstone seized his wrist, hauled him powerfully close, and clamped his own arm over Porrask's in a tight, punishing lock. Next moment he was dragging Porrask toward the door. Goggling, chattering spectators made way for them. Thunstone shouldered the door open and sprang out upon the paved yard in the cloudy light of evening, fetching Porrask with him.

Porrask blubbered a curse and strove to pull his prisoned arm free. Thunstone turned his own body and drove a shoulder up under Porrask's armpit. He slammed his back against Porrask's chest, then stooped forward with all his strength. Porrask came flying through the air above him and slammed down hard on the concrete.

The other customers had boiled out at the door of the Moonraven, all babbling at each other. Only Constance Bailey was silent, staring, scared. A loud, authoritative voice suddenly dominated the confusion:

"Now then, what's all this?"

It was Constable Dymock. Thunstone reflected that those words amounted almost to a ritual with British police.

Porrask got up slowly, unsteadily. He stood with bowed legs, and blinked at Thunstone, at Dymock. "This 'ere man attacked me," he blubbered. "Struck me."

"That's a lie," said Thunstone, the sharpest he had spoken so far to Porrask. "You tried to hit me, but I didn't lay a knuckle on you. If I had, you'd still be down on the ground."

"Let me tell you," said Constance Bailey quickly as she came toward them. "It was just the other way around, it was. Albert Porrask came to where I was sitting with Mr. Thunstone, and he spoke rude things, and when Mr. Thunstone objected, Albert Porrask tried to hit him."

"That's the right of it, Constable." It was Hawes speaking, from among the onlookers. "Mr. Porrask raised a disturbance in my place. I tried to calm him down and he shoved me. Whatever Mr. Thunstone did was in his own defense and in defense of Miss Bailey."

Dymock looked intently at Constance Bailey, but he spoke to Hawes. "Do you give him in charge?"

"That's for Mr. Thunstone to say," said Hawes. "He was the one attacked. Ask him."

"Mr. Thunstone?" prompted Dymock. He had moved closer to Constance Bailey. He looked as though he would put a protecting arm around her.

"No," said Thunstone, "I don't make any charge against him. He jumped on me, and I helped him off again. That's all."

Someone else came pushing through the circle of watchers. It was Ensley, his nostrils flaring, his eyes flashing like steel.

"Whatever sort of damned fool are you making of yourself, Porrask?" he demanded fearsomely.

"I didn't expect you'd know about this, sir," said Porrask, very timid now.

"I know all about you, everything you think and do, every instant," Ensley snapped, his face close to Porrask's. "They aren't going to arrest you, eh? All right, come along with me. You'd better make yourself understand that I have a special regard for Mr. Thunstone. Don't ever threaten him again."

The two walked off together, Ensley talking rapidly, Porrask silent, his head bowed.

"I'll just see you across to Mrs. Fothergill's, Connie," Dymock said, and Constance Bailey smiled up at him, and they, too, went away together.

Thunstone turned back to the door of the Moonraven, and Hawes came to his side. "I just want to get my cane," said Thunstone, "I left it at the table in here."

"Let me apologize for such a thing happening in any house of mine," Hawes said, "and I'm glad that all went as well as it did. If you'll allow me to say so, you can defend yourself proper."

"I've had to learn to do that," said Thunstone.

"Sir, would you take a drink with me, in my office?"

"I had a full pint of lager at supper," said Thunstone, "but, for the sake of good feeling, I'll take perhaps a half pint more."

"I keep a very good article of sherry," Hawes told him. "I'd be pleased if you'd try it and say what you think of it."

"A small one, then," said Thunstone.

They entered the Moonraven together.

# CHAPTER 7

Drops of rain spattered on Thunstone as he left the Moonraven, cane in hand, and hurried across Trail Street to Mrs. Fothergill's house. Two cars stood in front, small sedans, one recognizable as an English Ford. He opened the front door and there was Mrs. Fothergill in the hall, a fluttering vision of flowered frock and gleaming hair.

"Oh, Mr. Thunstone!" she hailed him, as though proclaiming his title before royalty. "Come in, come in, sir. Constance told me what happened, how fine it was in you to defend her."

"It was nothing at all," said Thunstone.

"No, but it was, it was brilliant. We've two couples staying here tonight, and both were at the Moonraven for dinner. They saw what happened. One couple—their name's Haring; they're Dutch as I believe—were a bit frightened. The others are named Inscoe; they're Americans like you, from a place called Ypsilanti. They were more amused than anything." She rolled up her eyes. "But both said you handled an unpleasant situation very well indeed."

"I always try to do my best, Mrs. Fothergill."

"Come into the drawing room here," she babbled, a white hand on his arm. "Do come in, why not? I can offer you a drink or something."

"Thank you, but no," he smiled. "There were whiskey and wine and brandy with Mr. Ensley at Chimney Pots, and at dinner I had a pint of lager, and later a sherry over there with Mr. Hawes. That's a great plenty for me in one day, but thank you again."

"But do come in and sit down a moment," she urged him. "Constance is in there; she wants so much to thank you again." She fairly towed him along by his arm and into the room where first he had paid for his accommodations. Constance Bailey sat rather limply in a chair. Dymock bent beside her. His hand was on the arm of the chair, close enough to her hand to take hold of it. He straightened up as he saw Thunstone.

"If you'll be all right now, Connie, I'll go my way," he said. "I daresay I should telephone some report of the matter to Gerrinsford, even though no charge is laid." He looked at Thunstone with frank admiration. "Sir, give me leave to say, you were in the right place at the right time this evening."

Away he went. Mrs. Fothergill's eyes followed him appreciatively.

"A splendid young man, Constable Dymock," she said. "He'll rise in his service. Connie, you could go farther and fare worse, you know."

"Oh, please, Mrs. Fothergill," protested Constance Bailey, not unhappily.

"In any case, he's got a regard for you," went on Mrs. Fothergill. "That's perfectly plain to see. But sit down with us, Mr. Thunstone, and you'd best change your mind about that drink."

"No, thank you, ma'am," said Thunstone as he found a chair. "But I'd like to ask a question or two."

"As many as you wish. Connie, you're still shaken, and you'll have something, at least. Sit where you are; I'll do the honors."

Mrs. Fothergill went to the sideboard and chose a bottle and two glasses. What she prepared was what Thunstone had seen Constance Bailey take at the Moonraven, gin and bitters. Carefully Mrs. Fothergill trickled drops from a tall flask labeled ANGOSTURA into one glass, then the other, twirling each so that the inside was filmed ruddily. Then she poured gin into the glasses, gave one to Constance Bailey, and sat down with her own.

"Now, sir," she smiled at Thunstone, "questions, that was your word, I believe."

"Forgive me if I seem to be prying, but why should Porrask hold such a grudge against Miss Bailey here?"

"Easily answered, that," said Mrs. Fothergill. "He'd wanted her to go out with him, and when she said him no, he didn't like that. He was even threatening to one or two young men who came to see her."

"Yes," contributed Constance Bailey. "He was a wild one, drinking deep and just working at this odd job and that before he had his garage. And when he drank he could be frightening—he can still be frightening. I didn't want to walk out with him, and that made him mad. He cursed me."

She drank rather deeply as she remembered.

"You call yourself a witch; didn't you curse him back?" asked Thunstone.

She shook her head and her fall of dark hair stirred. "I don't curse people. I've never gone into that kind of witchcraft."

"Albert Porrask was angry with her," contributed Mrs. Fothergill. "Angry and jealous. Constance hadn't been with me long, she was quite a young thing, and I felt that I was more or less her guardian. Porrask came here to the house to be ugly and bother her, and I showed him the door. He went away—he had to—but he's kept his grudge against Constance."

"I see," said Thunstone. "But he was mild enough tonight when Mr. Ensley spoke to him."

"He'd be mild to Mr. Ensley, right enough," said Mrs. Fothergill, sipping at her glass. "It was Mr. Ensley backed him to start his garage and machine-repair shop. As I hear it, Porrask had done some clever work with a car of Mr. Ensley's, and Mr. Ensley was glad for it and lent him money—I don't know just how much—so he could get into his own business. And Porrask has been pretty average glad to do what Mr. Ensley says, ever since."

"He was clearing the outlines on Old Thunder's image up on the slope this morning, and seemed to take orders from Mr. Ensley," said Thunstone.

"Why as to that, half the men in Claines do turns at shaping that figure each year at this time," Mrs. Fothergill told him. "Even some who are church members, attend St. Jude's, they're up there every time to do their part at it. And Mr. Gates doesn't like it, not a trifle."

"I gathered that Mr. Ensley is seriously interested in antiquities here," Thunstone said.

"Interested is the word for him," Mrs. Fothergill agreed. "He was at me for a bit, to tell him what I might know about the old history of Claines. But I didn't know much; my people never told me much. He talked to Connie once, that once and no more, though she knows a thing or two."

"Mr. Ensley says I study the wrong things," said Constance Bailey in a dull, timid voice.

"All this is interesting," said Thunstone frankly. "I might even say, important. Thank you, ladies, for talking to me."

"Turnabout's fair play, and fair play's a jewel," said Mrs. Fothergill, with what she must have meant for a winning smile. "Let me ask you a question in my turn. Just why have you come here?"

"I told you that when first we met; I've told several others since. I was curious about things I'd heard in London about Old Thunder and the turning of the Dream Rock," he replied. Rising, he brought out his notecase. "I want to pay for a few more days here. I've promised to attend church on Sunday, so I'll pay you up through Monday night."

Mrs. Fothergill thanked him for the money and entered the amount in her account book. He went up to his room and turned on the light. Rain scrabbled at the window pane, like tapping fingers. He went to the bathroom for a shower, donned pajamas and light cloth slippers and his robe, and returned along the hall. Behind another door he heard chattering voices; those would be more overnight guests. In his room again, he sat at the desk and filled more pages of his notebook with his observations of the evening.

Outside the window, the last light ebbed away. It rained in earnest now; it strained against the window, against the outer wall of the house. The ivy-cloaked tree swayed and gestured with its branches. Thunstone remembered a line from an old song, "The night wind waves its arms." The night had its own life, gave its own life to the world over which it ruled.

At last he finished his account of the day's events and set the notebook aside. He felt better after his hot shower. It soothed his body after the day's visit to Chimney Pots, the climbing of Sweepside, the strange moment of weakness at the bridge over Congdon Mire, the scuffle with Porrask at the Moonraven. This had been a fairly full day.

As he pondered, there came a knock at the door, a knock so

stealthy that he waited a moment before stepping there and opening. In slid Constance Bailey, so furtively that she seemed almost to tiptoe.

"I feel that I just must talk to you, Mr. Thunstone," she whispered. "It may be wrong, my coming to your room this way, but there are some things I just can't say in front of Mrs. Fothergill; she doesn't believe in things I know to be true."

"It's all right for you to come," he quickly reassured her. "Sit down and tell me whatever it is you feel like telling."

He resumed his chair beside the desk. She perched in the armchair and clenched her hands and crowded her feet close together.

"I don't really know how to begin," she almost bewailed.

"You might begin by telling me about yourself, and how you happen to be in Claines," he invited.

"That much won't take long."

And the story of her life, as she told it, was brief. She was not native to Claines; she had been born and brought up in Liverpool. Her parents were good to her, she said. They had been kind and had put her to school, where she did well in her classes. But when she was fifteen, they both had died. She had fallen into the hands of a stern spinster aunt, who had found Constance Bailey a job as a shop assistant in a place that sold china—hard work and fairly low pay. Mrs. Fothergill, visiting in Liverpool, had come into the shop, had fallen into conversation with Constance Bailey, had liked her, and had invited her to come and live in Claines and help around the house.

"She's been truly wonderful to me," said Constance Bailey. "The work isn't hard, and she doesn't treat me like a servant, more like a friend. That was six years ago I came, and I haven't been sorry for a moment."

Six years, said Thunstone to himself. Then she was only in her early twenties now. "You haven't said anything about witchcraft," he reminded.

"Oh," she said, "that started when I was quite little. I learned from my father's cousin—a man, a spiritist medium. That's how the craft is passed along, from a man to a woman, and then from the woman to another man."

"It's the same way in the American South," said Thunstone. "So he taught you your art, you say. Wasn't there more to it than the teaching? An initiation ceremony with a coven, and a sort of a confirmation?"

"I know what you mean," she said. "No, a white witch doesn't belong to a coven, a band of witches with a chief devil, all that black-magic part. I've heard the thing they do. The chief devil makes you put one hand under your feet, the other on top of your head, and swears you that all between your hands belongs to the ruler of hell." She shrugged, or perhaps she shivered. "I'd never do that, not for money. Nor go to their meetings, nor dance in their dances on a sabbat. Sabbat—that's a blasphemy, on the name of the holy Sab-bath."

"I don't think that's quite accurate," said Thunstone. "Ruth St. Leger-Gordon wrote that the word was French to begin with, *s'esbattre*, an old term that she says means to frolic. Now, in America they call a country dance a frolic, and they dance round and round, sometimes back to back like witches—what the dance-caller names a do-si-do." He smiled at her, trying to reassure. "I've danced at such frolics myself in the mountains, and never thought I was turning into a witch."

"I've never danced; I don't dance."

"So this is what you mean by being a white witch."

"Yes, it is. I only try to help people. The holy saints could do such things. I can cure warts and I can stop the blood from a running wound. I can draw out the fire from a burn by saying a text from the Bible—I must not tell you what it was, or it wouldn't work for me anymore. I've done things like that in Claines; I could take you to people who'd tell you."

"And your methods are secret?" he asked.

"They have to be, I say. I can't tell them, except to somebody I'm teaching, not if I want to keep my power. There's another Bible text to say when I stop the flow of blood. But now, if I cure people, make them well, it's no more a sin than if I was a doctor, is it?"

"Not that I can see," said Thunstone. "Let me tell you something else I've learned about witchcraft in the southern part of the States. Someone like you, who tries to do helpful things and combat evil, isn't called a witch, but a witch master or a witch mistress. I know one of the foremost of the witch masters over there. He has the same name as I do, John."

"John what?"

"The people just call him John. He's also a fine guitarist. You should hear him."

"Well, in any case, you're convinced that I'm good," said Constance Bailey. "You speak as though you trust me. Let me tell you how I feel about certain things here, and trust me in that as well."

"Of course."

"Well," she said again, and gestured with both hands. "It's always uncanny here in Claines, every year at the turning time for the Dream Rock, but this year it's worse than usual. Not everybody can feel it, but you said that you did. You said that last night you had a vision of what must have been other times here."

"Ancient times long dead," he said.

"No," she said. "No. Ancient times but not dead, not when they come to life in the night. You and I can see that, know that."

"Just the two of us?" he asked. "Nobody else? Not Mrs. Fothergill, for instance?"

"She laughs at me; she won't credit me when I talk about it. She says I dream it at night, in my sleep."

"How about somebody like Gram Ensley?" Thunstone suggested.

She creased her brow. "Now, you make me wonder about him. I can't properly say what he sees and knows, or doesn't. I told you that he asked me once about white witchcraft, then he told me that I was wrong, I was a fraud. Said I did my spells to cheat people. But I've never done that. Never asked a penny for anything else I did. I'm not a black witch."

"You truly believe what you're saying," said Thunstone.

"I have to believe. It's all in the Bible, about witches and spirits of the dead, so it has to be true. And at night this time of year, it's no dream, certainly. You felt it." She leaned forward. "You know it's not a dream. You know the house goes away all around, and strange things move." Her eyes grew wider. "It's dark now. If you should turn out your light here—"

"Suppose we turn it off and find out," he said suddenly.

"No, not for your life!" she squeaked. "Who knows what would happen?"

"Nobody will know what would happen if we don't find out." He studied persuasion into his voice. "You and I have had the experience, but both of us had it when we were alone. Mrs. Fothergill thought you were dreaming. I don't think I dreamed, but I wonder. If we turned out this light, and that other landscape came to us in the dark when we were together, we'd be sure of it."

"But it frightens me," she whimpered, her head sunk low, her face half-hidden in her dark flood of hair.

"Naturally it does, or you wouldn't have good sense. Let's try it, Miss Connie."

"Well, then." She lifted her head up. "Maybe I won't be so frightened if you're with me."

"I'll be with you every moment, and I'll be prepared."

He searched in his smaller satchel and brought out a flashlight no bigger than a fountain pen. This he clipped in the upper pocket of his robe.

"Constance Bailey," he said, "are you ready?"

"Yes, all right."

Thunstone sat on the edge of the bed. Constance Bailey came and sat close beside him. He could feel her body tremble.

"Now," he said, and put his hand to the light and turned the switch.

Darkness hurried through the air around them.

# CHAPTER 8

And Thunstone knew at once that he was somewhere outside, knew it as he had known it the night before. The rain that had clattered at the window was gone, and so was the window. Dimly he saw the landscape he had seen that previous night, dimly but more clearly than the first time. It was the place where Claines stood, but no Claines was there. Overhead winked stars, and the moon was only a curved scrap where it had been greatening to the full. And no street-lights on Trail Street, no Trail Street either. But he could see the dim, night-shadowed upward climb of Sweepside, and upon the surface there the outline of Old Thunder, with some sort of glow upon it to pick out the white perimeter.

"Constance," he said, "where are you? Do you see?"

"I can see," came her voice out of the dark beside him, smothered with awe. "You can see too, is that right?"

They were sitting together on a hummock of something, certainly not the bed. He lowered his hand to explore. It seemed to be rock, with a coating of what must be shaggy lichen. He turned and saw Constance Bailey there, a darker shape in the dimness. He felt her nervous grip upon his arm.

"We both see," he decided. "That means it's not imagination, not delusion. Not mass hypnotism; I've never believed in mass hypnotism, anyway. We both see what we see."

"This is Claines, but there's no Claines," she said. "Nor a house, not a street. We're in the open. I can see Old Thunder, shining like. And over there, where Chimney Pots ought to be—"

He looked in that direction.

Light showed over there, as of several ruddy fires. Around the fires clustered dark shapes, uncouth shapes even in the distance. He heard, far off, a jumble of voices, and they were not particularly merry voices. If they sang, they were discordant. He had time by now to feel that the air was chilly, not like July in Claines.

"Constance," he said, "listen carefully to what I say. I'm going out there to get a better look at what's going on."

"Oh no, don't!" she wailed, the words stumbling over each other.

"Listen carefully," he urged her again. "I'm only going to where I can see and hear them better. I won't go all the way, and I'll come back here to where we're sitting. This is the point where we must be when I turn on a light and fetch us back to our right time and place."

"Don't go," she besought him, and clung to his arm and shoulder.

"I'm going," he said, more sternly than he wanted. "But you stay here, right where you are. Don't move hand or foot until I come back."

"If you do come back!"

"I'll be coming back," he promised. "And when I call out to you, answer me loud and clear, to guide me again. Do you understand?"

"Ye-es."

"And you understand everything? And you'll do what I say?"

"Ye-es," again. "But—what if you don't come back?"

"I said I would, but, yes, suppose I don't. Here, take this."

He pushed the pencil flashlight into her hand. "Don't turn it on, not now. Just wait for me. Watch me the best you can in this darkness. You ought to be able to see my coming and going. But if something does happen to me and you think I can't make my way back, turn on that flashlight and then turn on the light in the room, and you'll be safe."

"Don't go," she pleaded again, almost tearfully.

"Stop talking like that," he commanded, and freed himself from her trembling hands. He rose to his feet and moved carefully in the gloom toward the fires and the chanting groups there.

He walked carefully, setting his feet flat to the ground, for he could feel a strew of pebbles under the thin soles of his slippers. He had no sense of being brave, though he did ask himself if he were not foolish. But Judge Pursuivant would approve of what he was doing, and so would Jules de Grandin, the brilliant little Frenchman he knew and admired. They, too, would want to see and hear and know. It was natural, it was human, to find things out. Mankind's poor underprivileged cousins, the apes and monkeys, had that prodding curiosity. And curiosity had grown into man's giant exploration of things, his search for the stuff of which reality is made, his will to cross oceans, cross space even, and find things out even while he dreamed of finding out more. Compulsive had to be the word, though Thunstone felt it was a word overused and misunderstood.

In the dark he came to what seemed to be the crest of a rise, and there he stopped. He strained his eyes to see what went on at those fires. The creatures there—they must be people—moved in a circle around the flickering flames. They moved in a ring. Thunstone remembered what he and Constance Bailey had talked about, witches dancing in a ring. If these people danced back to back, he could not see clearly. He did see that they tossed their arms. Several held long poles, perhaps spears.

They kept up a hubbub of voices. "Ohh, ohh, ohh," they seemed to chant. "Hai, hai, hai." Into their song came the sound of a thudding drum, and the bubbling skirl as of a wind instrument. Thunstone remembered the bone flute Ensley had shown him.

He had better come no closer, or he would lose his way back. He turned and tried to make out the lichen-shagged rock on which he had sat. "Constance!" he called loudly. "Constance Bailey!"

"Here, here," drifted back her voice.

At that, the singing by the fires beat up more strongly. Closer to Thunstone three figures bobbed into view. He could make out a shagginess to them, perhaps the clothes they wore. They stood for a moment; they seemed to peer in his direction. Then they moved purposefully toward him.

He backed away toward where Constance Bailey had hailed him. Once his foot slipped on a loose stone, his ankle almost turned. "Constance Bailey!" he called to her again.

"Here I am!"

At that, one of the approaching shaggy figures said something in a language he had never heard, and flexed itself and threw something.

The something whizzed close, struck earth with an abrupt whack. It was there almost against him, jutting upward. He seized it, dragged it free of the earth, and headed swiftly back. He came close enough to make Constance Bailey out, huddled on the boulder. He reached her side and sat down himself, then looked back along the way he had come.

The figures were approaching.

"Give me the light," he said, and took it from Constance Bailey's hand. He touched the switch, and his room sprang into view around him. Reaching for the light above his bed, he turned it on, and they were back in familiarity.

Rain clawed at the window, the rain that had not been there just now, when they had been outside in some other time of the world's long life. Again they sat together on the edge of the bed, Thunstone and Constance Bailey.

Still she cowered against him. Her trembling lips moved as though to form silent words. Perhaps she prayed.

"Steady," Thunstone urged her. "We're safe now. What I saw out there, in whatever long-ago time it was, looked like people dancing, sounded like people singing. But they're not out there now. The light brought us back here."

"The light," she echoed him. "The darkness—it was terrible."

"We're safe," he insisted. "Look here; they threw this at me."

He still held it in his hand, and he himself looked at it for the first time.

It was a spear, with a wooden haft nearly five feet long, straight as a ruler and oiled to darkness. Its point was of stone, beautifully chipped, a reddish quartz, perhaps jasper. The lashing was of stout, dull sinew.

"They threw it at me," he said again.

"They might have killed you."

"Well, it was dark out there for throwing." He got up and leaned the spear in a corner. "That came back from that ancient time, and it proves that we saw and heard and felt what we thought we did. Listen to me, Constance, don't mention this spear to anybody for the time being."

"I won't," she promised.

"And now you can go to your room, and see if you can get a night's rest."

"My room's up steps," she chattered. "A flight of stairs, and dark all the way up. I'm afraid."

"I'll come and stand at the foot, and shine my flashlight up for you," he offered. "When you're in the room, turn on your light and everything will be normal. Sleep with your light on if you want to."

"I will, and thank you."

"Don't thank me," he said.

"I do thank you, thank you for being what you are."

She went into the hall. He followed to where she opened a door that showed gloomy, steep steps. Standing there, he leveled the lean beam of his flashlight along the way she must climb. She mounted, not confidently, and opened a door above. He saw the light there as she turned it on. Then she closed her door and he returned to his own room. There he sat down to think.

What had it been, this experience? Time travel, as H. G. Wells had imagined it? If so, how did it work?

Because it had worked, with him and with Constance Bailey as a witness. He had been back in time and had returned, and yonder was a stone-headed spear to prove it.

Time travel had been a matter for speculation for many years. Theorists had considered it long before H. G. Wells had popularized it with his novel *The Time Machine*, published in 1895 as Thunstone remembered. He mused over the introduction to that curious tale, in which Wells had called time another dimension, had said that if man could somehow win free of his cramping world of length, breadth, and altitude he could travel in time, backward or forward. Here in Claines was no machine to take one through centuries. It seemed to be an accomplishment possible to only a few like himself and Constance Bailey, as extrasensory perception is the gift of only certain persons with a special aptitude.

Indeed, time travel might be something like extrasensory perception. Anyone could look back in memory to experiences of the past. And vividly you could imagine, rationalize the future—choose a

winner in a race, divine a course of action that would bring you a
success in a day or a year. And your dreams, they could give you a
glimpse of the long ago. Maybe they even gave you glimpses of the
future, those visions of tremendous, intricate cities, with the air
crystal clear above remote towers, strange traffic on strange streets.

If he had been able to journey through time, what time was it he
had seen here, under the conditions that must be right for it? The
immemorial past, before ever there was a Claines? He had seen Old
Thunder in that strange time. Or might it be a distant future when
the houses of Claines had been rubbed away from their landscape,
but when Old Thunder still showed there?

Possibilities were infinite. Jakob Böhme had said that anything was
possible, even the most bizarre improbability. Thunstone yawned. He
decided to leave his light on, as he had advised Constance Bailey to
leave hers on. He went sound asleep under its glow.

If he dreamed, he did not remember dreaming when he woke next
morning. He turned off the light and looked at his watch; it was half-
past seven, as it had been when he had wakened the day before. The
rain had gone; the sun was bright at his window. He donned his robe
and went out and to the bathroom door, but it was locked and he
could hear running water inside. He returned to his room, filled and
smoked a pipe, then sought the bathroom again. Now it was empty.
He showered quickly, brushed his teeth and shaved, and returned to
his room to dress.

Downstairs, he found Mrs. Fothergill in her sitting room. She held
a cigarette in her left hand, its filter daubed with lipstick, and in her
right she cuddled a cup.

"Have a coffee with me, Mr. Thunstone?" she greeted him. "It's
yet a few minutes to eight and our other guests aren't down for
breakfast." She set down her cup, lifted the pot from the side table
and filled another cup for him. Thanking her, he sat and sipped.
Again he reflected that Mrs. Fothergill, at least, provided good coffee
in England.

"It's turned out to be a lovely morning," she said. "Did that storm
keep you awake last night?"

"No, not much," he replied. "I turned in fairly early and slept straight through."

"I'm glad to hear you say so. My own rest was a good one, but poor Connie seems to have had a restless night. She has such strange imaginings."

Noise of feet on the stairs, and a couple entered, then another. Mrs. Fothergill twittered at them hospitably.

"Good morning, good morning!" she cried. "Mr. and Mrs. Haring, and Mr. and Mrs. Inscoe—"

Thunstone was on his feet as Mrs. Fothergill made introductions. The Harings were taffy-haired, pink-faced, spruce; they looked as though they might be blood relatives instead of husband and wife. The Inscoes were older and wore American sports clothes. Inscoe was bald in front and had immense silver-rimmed spectacles. Mrs. Inscoe looked rather gaunt and intense, and wore her dull black hair in a bushy bob. They asked polite questions. Thunstone told them that he lived in New York but had been in Michigan several times, had visited Ypsilanti. He mentioned two professors at Eastern Michigan University there, friends and correspondents of his, but the Inscoes had never heard of either of them.

Breakfast was served them by Constance Bailey, looking rather wan. She spoke in a tired whisper to answer Mrs. Fothergill, and looked at Thunstone only a single time, at once stealthily and admiringly.

Haring enthusiastically praised what he ate, the fried egg, the toast and jelly, the links of sausage. He declared that breakfast was a meal greatly esteemed in the Netherlands, and sought to explain a sort of pancake, complete with bacon fried into it, which he called *spekpannekoken*. When Mrs. Fothergill displayed interest in this dish, Mrs. Haring told her in accented detail the method of mixing and preparing it. Mrs. Fothergill only blinked her eyes as she listened. Inscoe, too, ate all that was served him, but his wife ate only the egg and toast liberally jellied. To Thunstone she confided that she did not eat meat, and added that the world's great thinkers and planners practiced a like abstention.

Breakfast over, the Inscoes hurried their luggage into the hired

Datsun and went bustling away—to Bath, Thunstone thought they said. The Harings lingered and walked outside with Thunstone. From the yard they gazed up to where, on Sweepside, two dogs showed where a pair of workers busied themselves at redefining the outlines of Old Thunder.

"Now, sir, that is an amazing grotesque," declared Haring to Thunstone. "What might it be called?"

"Its name is Old Thunder, and each year at this time they dig its outline clear again, to let the chalk show through," said Thunstone. "Nobody knows how old that image is, only that it seems to go back before history."

"Indeed so? I feel an impulse to climb up there and see it at the closer quarters."

"I'm afraid that it's on jealously guarded private property," Thunstone felt it necessary to say. "The owner has posted signs to warn trespassers away, and he has a harsh word for those who do come up without his say-so."

"Ah? Then I think we go somewhere else. The Roman Wall, perhaps. That is not forbidden to the public."

The Harings energetically loaded their bags into their car. Thunstone made his way across Trail Street and along past the shops that had become familiar to him. He went into the post office to mail his letters and to buy a small pouch of smoking tobacco. The postmistress called him by name and asked him how he was enjoying his stay. It seemed to him that he was accepted in Claines.

Outside the post office, he met Dymock, who pushed along his bicycle as usual.

"Good morning, Mr. Thunstone," Dymock greeted him. "If I may say so, I'm glad that last night's little matter turned out with no more trouble. Albert Porrask got a lesson he's needed for some little while. I made a report on the matter to headquarters and was told to set it down as terminated."

"It's terminated as far as I'm concerned," nodded Thunstone. "Tell me, how did you rest last night?"

"Rest last night?" Dymock said after him. "As it so happens, not very well. Late on, about half an hour to midnight, a big van stalled on

Trail Street; it slewed around so as to block the way. I was out there to see that it got back in action, and then I was wakeful and walked here and there in the dark to wear myself out so I could sleep."

"You say you were in the dark. How did the town look to you?"

"About as usual," said Dymock. "There was quite a shower of rain, and the clouds up there to hide what would have been a fine moon."

"And all the houses were there as usual?" asked Thunstone. "The whole town as you know it?"

Dymock smiled in his mustache. "You've been talking to Connie Bailey, is that it? She told you her imaginings?"

"Well," said Thunstone, "she has mentioned something."

Dymock's smile vanished. "I could wish for her sake that she didn't have those dreams or visions or whatever they are. She worries Mrs. Fothergill, too. I can't think that such fancies are good for her."

"Then you don't believe in them," said Thunstone.

"My training is to believe in facts, sir," replied Dymock. "She thinks she sees these things at night, but I know I don't see them. And I'm concerned for her. I've never said so much in the subject to anyone before, and I trust you not to repeat our conversation to her."

"Naturally I won't. But let me ask you, how do you explain dizziness on that bridge over Congdon Mire, and why it's apt to happen at the time of turning the Dream Rock?"

"I don't explain it," said Dymock flatly. "That's something that awaits explanation. Perhaps a psychologist could help there, but I'm no psychologist, only a policeman. And that can be quite a line of work."

"I'm sure of that," said Thunstone.

They took leave of each other. Thunstone headed on toward St. Jude's. He saw David Gates on the lawn, scratching with a hoe around some rose bushes. He turned in at the walk and approached the curate.

"Ah, Mr. Thunstone," said Gates, straightening up, the hoe in his heavy hand. "You see, I do my own gardening here."

"Those roses are beautiful," said Thunstone. "I wouldn't have bothered you, but questions keep rising about this little hamlet of Claines."

"Questions?"

"For one," said Thunstone, "how did you sleep last night?"

"Why, fairly well. I lay for a while and thought about a point or two in my sermon tomorrow, matters of emphasis."

"You lay in the dark?" asked Thunstone.

"Naturally I did. I find that thinking in the dark is often profitable."

"And did you have any peculiar sensations?" was Thunstone's next question.

Gates laughed at that, quietly but loftily. "You wonder if the approach of the turning of the Dream Stone affects my imagination. No, sir, not in the least. I leave that to one or two residents here subject to illusion, and I take it you've talked to them."

"I've talked to Constance Bailey," said Thunstone.

"Constance Bailey," Gates said the name after him. "Now, there's an unhappy young woman who lets her fancies run away with her. I've tried to reason with her, not very successfully. Once or twice, I've wondered if she weren't in the habit of taking some sort of harmful drug. Frankly, Mr. Thunstone, I see nothing in her extravagances of talk, and I've been glad that lately she hasn't come to me with them."

"I must say that I rather like her," said Thunstone. "She works for Mrs. Fothergill, and she's helpful and mannerly. But another thing interests me. It's about the stream yonder, what's called Congdon Mire."

"That grimy flow?" Gates turned to look eastward in the direction of Congdon Mire. "I consider it a hazard to the health of this locality. I wish it could be drained."

"Did you ever walk on the bridge there and feel a dizziness?"

"Ah, so you've heard that superstition too? No, I've never felt any such thing. More imagination here and there, I should say, perhaps helped along by generous potations at one or other of our pubs here."

"I felt a dizziness there yesterday," Thunstone told him. "I nearly fell in. And I hope you'll believe that I hadn't been drinking. I hear that that sensation comes at Congdon Mire at the time of the stone turning."

"I deplore such superstitions," vowed Gates. "If you come to church tomorrow, you'll hear me say so in no uncertain terms."

"I've said that I'd be there, and look forward to your sermon."

Gates turned back to his roses, and Thunstone walked back again toward the center of town.

As he trudged along, a shout hailed him. It came from the yard of Chimney Pots.

Three figures stood there. Close to Trail Street, Hob Sayle tinkered with a lawn mower. Farther in on the grass stood Gram Ensley and Porrask, and Ensley waved vigorously for Thunstone to cross over and join them.

# CHAPTER 9

Thunstone waited for a shabby light truck to pass, then hurried across busy Trail Street. Hob Sayle shoved his lawn mower along, not glancing up. Thunstone came to where Ensley and Porrask stood waiting.

Ensley wore the same jacket as yesterday, or perhaps another of the same cloth and cut. His necktie looked like those worn by the Brigade of Guards, and Thunstone wondered if he was entitled to wear it. Ensley smiled hospitably. Porrask, in stained denims, hunched his burly shoulders and lowered his eyes shyly.

"Mr. Thunstone, you've become a familiar sight on our street," Ensley greeted him. "I hope you like it in Claines."

"I'm beginning to feel acquainted here," said Thunstone. "I said I'm beginning to feel it. It would take a long while to claim the whole feeling."

He glanced at Porrask, who grunted noncommittally.

"I venture to trust you've forgiven Porrask here," said Ensley. "I'm aware that he's sometimes gruff to strangers, but he says he knows you now."

"And that's the truth, sir; there it is," said Porrask, not happily. "No hard feelings, I 'ope, sir."

"None on my part," Thunstone assured him at once.

"Meanwhile, Mr. Thunstone, have you been comfortable here?" inquired Ensley. "Did you rest well last night?"

"Oh, fairly well," replied Thunstone. "After I got to sleep."

"Then you must have lain awake, I hazard."

"I was awake, but I didn't lie there long," said Thunstone. "I was up. I studied over some of the things you and I have talked about.

About Claines, for instance, and how it might date back, if we could arrive at dates, to the Stone Age."

He lounged on his cane to say that. Ensley eyed the cane and then eyed Thunstone.

"The Old Stone Age," Ensley said, as though to correct him. "The Rough Stone Age, the Paleolithic. The age of man's greatest advance. I've told you that I've been selfish enough to discourage any digs and explorations here by universities and government groups. Selfish, I say —I want to do my own assessments. I believe in clinging to ancient customs, ancient traditions. Without the past, what would the present be? That's why I promote the annual refinishing of Old Thunder on the slope over there; that's why I approve of the annual turning of the Dream Rock."

"The Dream Rock," said Thunstone after him. "Do you suppose the Dream Rock can give dreams in Claines?"

"What sort of dreams might you mean?" asked Ensley, almost sharply.

"Possibly dreams of those prehistoric times you're talking about," said Thunstone.

Ensley looked at him searchingly. So did Porrask.

"Dreams, or perhaps visions," elaborated Thunstone. "Glimpses of what this place once was like, long ago."

Ensley still stared. "Have you had such dreams?" he almost prodded at Thunstone.

"I suppose I have, in a way. I find my imagination roused here. Perhaps talking with you has helped it along."

"Dreams," said Porrask, from where he stood apart. "I don't dream any great lot, myself. Work 'ard in the day, sleep sound in the night. That's been my way of it."

"I've heard a great psychologist say that we all dream," said Ensley, "and that those who say they don't dream, only dream and forget that they've dreamed."

That sounded like one of his snubs for Porrask. Thunstone thought for a moment before speaking.

"Dreams are unsubstantial things," he said then. "But what if somebody dreamed of wandering among flowers, for instance, and dreamed that he picked a flower, and then woke up with the flower in his hand?"

Ensley started visibly. "Don't tell me you've woken up here with a flower in your hand."

"No," said Thunstone gently. "No flower."

He gazed up the long pitch of Sweepside. "Ever since you brought up the subject," he said, "I've thought a great deal about the people who lived here back then, all those thousands of years back into the Paleolithic."

"Ten thousand years ago," nodded Ensley, and he seemed more calm. "It was ten thousand years ago, say the archaeologists, that Jericho was built. The first city, as far as research can establish."

"The Book of Genesis tells us that Cain built the first city, and named it Enoch after his son," said Thunstone.

"Come, surely you're not a fundamentalist, are you? Well, maybe Enoch was another name for Jericho. Twenty-five hundred people lived in the beginning at Jericho, they estimate. But ten thousand years ago, there was a community living here, and maybe seventy-five people living in it." Ensley gazed over the housetops of Claines. "They lived here and built houses. Wooden walls plastered with clay, and pitched roofs with thatches. Houses like that probably would look pretty much like home, even to the eyes of moderns."

"Do you suppose they farmed?" asked Thunstone. "Did they harvest grain? The people at Jericho seem to have done that."

Ensley tossed his head, as though impatient at the question. "That was down in Asia Minor where it was warm. The Neolithic Age had begun there, with all its advances and alterations in culture. Up here, the Ice Age was receding, but it was still much colder than it is today. But even so, the people here were wise according to their lights."

"You sound as though you knew them," said Thunstone.

"I've tried my best to know them. They were building toward what we mistakenly call civilization."

"Amen to that," said Thunstone. "I read a book some years ago, a collaboration as I remember, that referred all our modern knowledge to visitors from outer space. In one place, their book said outright that both the Neanderthal and Cro-Magnon races were brutes."

"Brutes?" snapped Ensley. "Just who were those authors?"

"I have to admit, I've forgotten."

"Then you've well forgotten them," pronounced Ensley. "We think we tower so high. We only stand on the shoulders of those wise ancient people, who began all our knowledge for us."

"Amen," agreed Thunstone again. "I go along with my friend Jean Stuart, who visited those Stone Age caves in France and Spain, where the cave paintings are."

"Yes," said Ensley, "you've mentioned her name, I remember."

"She wrote frankly that she felt those cave dwellers had as great minds as we have today; that they must have been philosophers, rationalists, as well as fine artists. I've always wondered why we don't find cave paintings like those, here in England."

"Maybe such things haven't been discovered as yet," said Ensley, rather darkly. "At least, they've not been brought to public attention. The only recorded example I know of is in Wales, in a cave picturesquely called Bacon's Hole, where there's a sort of grid pattern of ten bars of bright red paint of some sort. Ten bars, one above the other. What would you make of that, Mr. Thunstone?"

"I'd be only guessing, but I'd say that whoever painted that pattern of bars understood the decimal system in mathematics. He'd seem to be recording in tens."

"As in ten thousand years," said Ensley, dreamily this time.

"You appear to like the number ten thousand," ventured Thunstone.

"Maybe I do like it; it's a good, solid, round number. I must say, I'm glad of your conversation whenever I have a chance at it. I'd judge that you have a considerable gift of perception. So few have that."

"I think that Constance Bailey has something of perception," Thunstone said.

"That little fraud doesn't enter this discussion," snapped Ensley. "Before I'm done, I hope to see her driven out of Claines, and her witch pretenses with her."

Porrask heaved his shoulders again. Maybe he sighed.

"And you, Mr. Ensley," Thunstone changed the subject. "Do you ever have the sort of dream or vision of the past we've been talking about?"

"See here, aren't you tired of standing about in the yard?" asked Ensley suddenly. "Why don't we go inside, you and I, and get on with our discussion? There's a great deal we'd like to hear from each other."

"Thanks, I'd like to, but I'm going to catch the bus to London," said Thunstone, deciding even as he spoke.

"London?" repeated Ensley. "Surely you aren't leaving Claines just now?"

"No, I expect to return sometime this evening."

"Good, good," said Ensley. He put a hand on Thunstone's arm. "I'd be greatly disappointed if you left us and didn't come back. Let me invite you to dinner tomorrow noon, here at Chimney Pots."

"I've promised to attend church at St. Jude's tomorrow."

"That's all right, but dinner after church. Shall we say one-thirty? There's someone I want you to meet, and I think there'll be things to interest you."

"Why," said Thunstone, "I'll accept, and thank you very much."

He walked away. He knew that Ensley watched him as he went, and that Porrask watched, too.

At Mrs. Fothergill's, he went upstairs to his room. Constance Bailey was there, tidying.

"I'm glad to see you," he said quickly. "I'm going to be gone for a while—for some hours, at least—and I want to hide this."

He went to the corner where he had leaned the stone-headed spear. "Could you keep it in your room?" he asked.

"Oh, I wouldn't dare!" she cried, shaking her head so that her hair tossed. "That's an evil thing, Mr. Thunstone; it's a bad thing—"

"Well then, we'll hide it here, in the bed."

The bed was already made. He swept back the coverlet and the top sheet and laid the spear flat on the bottom sheet, with its head tucked under the pillow. He drew the bedclothes over it, and Constance Bailey helped with hands that shook. When they had smoothed the coverlet down, nobody could have told that the spear was there.

"Do you truly think you should?" she asked.

"I think I must; I don't want anyone to know about it just yet. Now, good bye for the present."

"Mr. Thunstone," she said, her voice wretchedly shaking, "do you think you're doing a good thing here, with so much danger around and about?"

"There's always danger," he said, "at every point in our lives."

"But this," she said, "this going back into the long ago, all among those savage people. What if you go back again and they kill you?"

"I hope they won't, but what if they do?"

She seemed to sway before him, she almost staggered. "Aren't you afraid of death, Mr. Thunstone?"

He looked at her. He smiled, and shook his big dark head.

"No," he said, "I'm not. That doesn't mean I want to die—if I wanted that, I'd be crazy. But I'm not afraid of death. Several times I've come close to death, and I was never afraid, not any of the times. Why, Connie? Are you afraid?"

"Yes, I am," she whispered. "Thinking of it makes me run all cold inside. I don't know what will happen after I'm dead. Maybe nothing will happen."

"Maybe nothing will happen," he repeated the words. "Of course, we don't know. There are lots of promises about an afterlife, but we don't know what they mean. But anyway, I'm not afraid of death. I can't afford to be."

She gazed at him as though she tried to comprehend.

"But what if there's nothing?" she asked him after a moment.

"Then it will be like going to sleep, I suppose. And some of the happiest times I've known have been spent in sleep."

"Then you're not afraid," she said, almost an accusation.

"No, by God, I'm not. There just isn't any future in being afraid of death. So don't you be afraid, either." He turned toward the door. "Good bye," he said again.

"Good bye," she said again, as though saying it forever.

Cane in hand, he hurried downstairs and across Trail Street to the Moonraven. Hawes lounged in the parking lot.

"Good morning, sir," he said. "We don't open till eleven."

"I wondered when the next bus to London stopped here," said Thunstone.

"Next bus to London? Ten-thirty, if it's on time, and most days it is."

Thunstone glanced at his watch. It was just ten o'clock. "I'll have to telephone," he said.

"Call box right there, in front of the post office," Hawes told him, pointing.

Thunstone hurried to it. He fumbled out coins and rang a number at the University of London, the office of Leslie Spayte. A deeply drawling voice answered.

"Yes? Professor Spayte here."

"This is John Thunstone. I'm glad I could catch you in your office, Professor."

"I'm more or less always in my office, even on a Saturday. What can I do for you, Thunstone?"

"You can talk to me, and hear me talk. I'm catching the ten-thirty bus here in Claines. I should be there in two hours, as I figure."

"Why not a spot of lunch?" asked Spayte. "Why not meet me at a pub where we've been together before, the Friend at Hand in Herbrand Street? Say one o'clock, or thereabouts?"

"Fine, that's one of my favorite pubs," applauded Thunstone. "I wish we could have Philo Vickery along. He'd appreciate a few of the things I have to tell."

"As it happens, I'd say we can have him," drawled Spayte. "He was in here just now—full of wild surmises as usual, like stout Cortez's men silent upon a peak in Darien, though it must have been Balboa if they gazed on the Pacific. Even Keats could be wrong sometimes. Anyway, Vickery left to go to the bookstore, Dillon's. Seems that one of his nightmarish books is on sale there and he wonders how it's going. But he'll be coming back. If you can be at the Friend at Hand at one o'clock, I'll just fetch him along."

"Great. I'll see you."

"I'll count the minutes. All right, Thunstone."

A click as Spayte hung up.

Thunstone went back to the door of the Moonraven. Hawes remarked that it was a fine day, but that last night's rain would be a help to the crops. He went on to say that he was glad for Thunstone to put Albert Porrask in his place the night before, that it would take Porrask months to get shirty again. When Thunstone guardedly mentioned the possibility of night visions at the time of the turning of Dream Rock, Hawes said that only Constance Bailey had cloth-headed notions like that. The bus rolled in and stopped, and Thunstone got aboard and paid his fare to London.

He sat by a window and watched Trail Street trundle past, watched Congdon Mire slide under, watched the country beyond. It was like leaving a place he had lived in for years to get away from Claines. The bus purred to a stop at Gerrinsford, where people got off and more people got on. A pudgy old man in a tan suit came to sit beside Thunstone and speak to him with ready friendship about the fineness of the weather. When Thunstone replied, the man asked if he were a Scot.

"I'm American," said Thunstone.

"Oh, ah," said the other. "You're of such a fine height, I thought Scot. Now America, there's a land I hope to visit one day."

He went on to say that his daughter had gone there, that she had married a man from Texas, that her son was in the United States Army. Rattling on, he mentioned the ancient friendship between England and the United States, asked Thunstone about income tax in America, and when Thunstone explained as best he could, wished earnestly that taxes in England were as low.

As they talked, the bus cruised through other towns, stopping to let passengers off or take passengers on. Nine came and went, and they rolled through the streets of London, at last coming to the terminal at Victoria Station.

Everyone got off. Thunstone said good bye to his seatmate and sought the underground station. Far below the earth, he waited for his train and rode away northward.

He changed at Green Park, passed the stations at Piccadilly Circus, Leicester Square, and Holborn, and got off at Russell Square. There was an escalator to ride up and up a tall, cliff like slope; then a walk to a heavily grilled door and another ascent in a crowded elevator like a soaring freight car and at last the open air of London on the street.

It was a street that Thunstone knew, not far from his hotel on Southampton Row. He walked a few yards and turned left into Herbrand Street.

That was more like an alley, a narrow, seamed pavement between buildings closely crowding on either hand. As before, he wondered how one car could safely pass another there. On ahead of him rose a sign he recognized, painted in tawny yellow on blue-green. It depicted a rescuer leaning down from an open boat to reach and help an understandably desperate flounderer in tossing waves. The door of the place displayed above it, in raised, gilded letters, the name THE FRIEND AT HAND. To the left of that, more letters promised SPLENDID FOOD, and to the right, EXCELLENT ALES.

Thunstone entered a spacious room amid a hubbub of voices. The Friend at Hand was always thronged at lunchtime. Customers lined the bar, besieged the long buffet on the far side of it. He stood for a moment, looking here and there. Then a voice rose to shout his name.

At a table on a sort of raised platform in the left rear corner sat his friends Spayte and Vickery, both lifting their arms to wave a greeting to him.

# CHAPTER 10

Thunstone flung up his own right arm to acknowledge the salutation. Then he worked his way through the considerable crowd to a place against the bar. A white-jacketed barman looked up and saw him.

"Oh, you're back in town, sir," he said. "Missed you here."

"I've been in the country for a few days," said Thunstone. "Let me have a pint of the special bitter."

The bartender drew it. Thunstone put down a pound note and went up two steps to where Spayte and Vickery sat, smiling their welcome. Spayte was impeccable in tailored gray, and gray was his close-curled hair. His beard was trimmed to a smart point, his mustaches carefully waxed. As often before, Thunstone thought he had an Elizabethan look. Vickery was considerably younger, leaner, than Spayte. He was dressed in an open-fronted jeans jacket and a blue T-shirt which bore on its front the cryptic word LATER. He had the face of an Indian warrior, with gaunt cheeks, straight nose, strong chin. His dark hair was swept back from a broad, high brow, and fell on either side to his square shoulders.

"On time to the dot," Spayte greeted Thunstone. "One o'clock, as I believe I said. And one o'clock it is."

"You said one o'clock or thereabouts," said Thunstone, setting down his mug. "I see that both of you are eating. Give me a minute to get myself something."

The buffet, too, had its crowd of customers. Thunstone chose a long sausage of a kind he had learned to like, a scoop of salad, and some white bread and butter. He carried the food back to where Spayte and Vickery were eating. Spayte had a slice of quiche. Vickery had taken a generous wedge of liver pâté and a Scotch egg, both of which he ate with good appetite, and drank from his mug of dark beer. Thunstone sat down and began on his own lunch.

"I got your letter from there in Claines," said Spayte. "That little place isn't hospitable to scholars, and so I haven't gone there as yet. Like Alan Breck Stewart, I'm no very keen to stay where I'm no wanted. How have you fared there?"

"That's what I came to tell," said Thunstone. "Claines is jumping with uncanny things."

"You wrote me nothing about those," said Spayte. "You should have done, I'm interested in Claines, however inhospitable."

"Fine ale, this," said Vickery, drinking. "Excellent, as promised on the sign outside. Even George Borrow would approve." Then he looked sharply at Thunstone. "Uncanny, did you say uncanny? Why haven't you told us before?"

"I'm not surprised to see that word fetch him," said Spayte to Thunstone. "You know that the uncanny is his enthusiasm, and he writes it into his books. He's been at me the last day or so with something he came on at the Museum library, all about old churches being built on the sites of abandoned pagan temples, and what it means, at least to him. For my part, I've forgotten what it may mean, if anything."

"Our professor here is rock-ribbedly empirical," said Vickery affectionately. "Believes only in material evidence, and decides for himself what the material evidence is."

"I've always been glad to hear him talk on any subject," said Thunstone.

"I also, because then I can disagree each time," said Vickery. "I wouldn't be without him, Thunstone; he's a fascinating character. I'd put him in a novel, only I'm afraid he'd bring an action for damages."

"What damages?" wondered Spayte. "What could you write that could damage me? But hold on; we're interrupting Thunstone here. What's the uncanniness you say you've found in Claines?"

"I'll tell you about that," said Thunstone, and as they ate their lunches and drank from their mugs, he did so.

He did his best to omit nothing. He told about the Moonraven and Mrs. Fothergill's bed-and-breakfast enterprise, about St. Jude's and the opinions of David Gates, about Chimney Pots and Gram Ensley, about the ancient chalk outline of Old Thunder on Sweepside and the fallen pillar called the Dream Rock and the traditional activities at both of them. He described, too, his grapple with Porrask, at which Vickery remarked, "Well done," and told of Ensley's courteous but cryptic manner and speech, and finally of his sense of seeing and feeling a strange landscape at night.

They listened with great attention, and when he had finished they made eager comments.

"This dream or nightmare you had, now—" began Spayte.

"It wasn't a dream, and I can prove it," interrupted Thunstone, somewhat impatiently. "I told you I brought back a Stone Age spear from it, a spear that was used to threaten me. I can show you that. But in any case, a man knows the difference between a dream and a reality."

"I don't," vowed Vickery. "Quite often, I wonder if life itself isn't a dream, and a thoroughly unpleasant one most of the time."

"I believe that of you, Vickery, and Sigmund Freud himself would be puzzled by your dreams," said Spayte. "But you're into the supernatural here, Thunstone old man, and I'm not a good friend to the supernatural."

"Supernatural is the laziest word in the vocabulary of ignorance," put in Vickery. "Nothing is supernatural, because nothing can transcend the laws of nature. Don't glitter at me like that, Herr Professor; I'm only quoting from Louis K. Anspacher. I don't know much about him, but I liked that statement of his enough to commit it to memory."

"Touché, so I'll change the word to supernormal," said Spayte. "Let me ask you a cheeky question, Thunstone, and you can answer it or not as you choose. Do you take drugs of any sort?"

"Not the kind you mean," replied Thunstone, with a grin. "The only narcotics I ever use, and I try to use them temperately, are alcohol, tobacco, tea, and coffee."

"All good of their kind," said Vickery approvingly. "Let me say something, Thunstone. I believe your whole story, believe it implicitly, and I can offer a good precedent for evidence of journeying back to the past."

"What sort of precedent, for God's sake?" demanded Spayte.

"It's in a very interesting book called *An Adventure,* and there's an equivocal title for you, I grant, but it tells about an adventure, right enough. It seems that in 1901 there were two highly intelligent and deeply respected English schoolmistresses, Anne Moberly and Eleanor Jourdan, who visited Versailles and went into the Trianon gardens, where the French court liked to amuse itself before the Revolution wiped out the court and the courtiers, at the end of the eighteenth century."

"Yes, of course," said Thunstone, interested. "I've read about that. There have been some interesting articles."

"I've seen the book myself, some years back," added Spayte, finishing his quiche.

"And I happen to own a copy, edition of the 1930s," continued Vickery. "Let me just summarize for you. These ladies—and I say again, they came from distinguished families of educators and churchmen—well then, they walked into the Trianon gardens, not paying attention to which way they took, and they found themselves among people in eighteenth century costumes."

"Masqueraders," growled Spayte in his beard.

"Yes, that's been charged," said Vickery, unabashed. "They spoke to some of these in French, and found the conversations more or less mystifying. They crossed a bridge, over a ravine where a cataract flowed, and at last they came back among scenes and people of their own time, the beginning of the twentieth century."

"I remember some of those details," nodded Thunstone, but Spayte kept a gloomy silence.

"All right then," went on Vickery, "these two ladies came away wondering exactly what it was they had seen. They wrote out their impressions, both of them. They studied maps of Trianon, and didn't understand. Buildings on the map didn't agree with the buildings they had seen on their walk; some seemed to have been moved, some seemed to have disappeared."

"The accounts I've seen had maps to demonstrate that," said Thunstone. Spayte still was silent.

"They brought their accounts to show to the SPR, the Society for Psychical Research," Vickery warmed to his story. "Had they journeyed into the past, they wondered. The SPR brushed them off. In those days, it included distinguished scholars like Sir William Crookes, like Sir Oliver Lodge. People who read their accounts said they were all wrong, especially about the ravine and the cataract and the bridge, none of which existed in the Trianon gardens at the time of that visit in 1901. And that sort of disbelief went on after they published the first edition of their written recollections."

"Yes, that's right," said Thunstone. "They did a lot of research, carloads of it. They even identified people they'd met on their walk, gave their names as courtiers and servants of the year 1789, isn't that the date?"

"So they did," said Spayte. "They even purported to have seen Marie Antoinette."

"And finally," said Vickery, "after their book had been published and pretty much derided by all the reviewers who cared to notice it at all—after they'd been accused of having illusions, perhaps of making up the whole story—a map turned up, in 1913 as I remember, an old lost map crumpled and stuffed up a chimney in a house where Jean-Jacques Rousseau had lived. And that map showed the gardens as those two ladies had seen it in 1901 and as it had been in 1789—all the buildings in their 1789 places, and it included the vanished ravine and the bridge and so on."

Triumphantly Vickery spread his hands, with a fragment of his Scotch egg in one of them. "And since then," he said, "there's been a whole lot of taking back of all the sneers and charges."

"So I've heard," said Thunstone. "What's your opinion, Spayte?"

"It's certainly an interesting story," replied Spayte. "A curious one. And I'm afraid I must reserve judgment."

"Which means, you're afraid to give the right answer to the thing," charged Vickery good-humoredly.

"I don't know where to go for a logical answer," said Spayte.

"Try going to Einstein," urged Vickery. "To Einstein's theory of relativity, and what J. W. Dunne calls serialism. The point they make is, we're cramped into a three-dimensional world. We experience it only instant by instant of time."

"Thomas de Quincey had one of his opium dreams about that," said Spayte. "About a water clock, and drops passing through, a hundred of them every second. When the fiftieth drop was on its way through, forty-nine drops didn't exist because they were gone, and fifty more drops didn't exist because they were yet to come. That's the way it happens here with us, a hundredth of a second at a time. That's what time is, a scrap of a second."

"But time exists," Vickery pursued, "so that if we can get out of our three dimensions into the fourth dimension of time—"

"Yes, yes," broke in Spayte impatiently. "I've heard that all, many times before. Thunstone says he got into it in the dark. But surely, Thunstone, there are lights all over this little village of yours."

"They have streetlights all along their main way, Trail Street, and in shops and houses," said Thunstone. "But when I turn out the light in my room it's full darkness there, and then the other landscape comes back, all dark night except for stars overhead, and no village at all."

Spayte tweaked his elegant beard. "Thunstone, you know by now how much I like you," he said. "You've been entertained at my home, and my wife rhapsodizes about you until I begin to be jealous. But I must protest against these imaginings. Imagination can't come into something like this."

"Can it not?" said Vickery, his warrior face seamed into a smile. "I've read the statement of a great, great man that imagination is more important than knowledge."

Spayte swung his own face toward Vickery. "What's that you're saying? Whoever offered such drivel as that?"

"I can answer that," said Thunstone, himself smiling. "It was written by someone we've just been discussing—Albert Einstein, in an essay he called 'On Science.' It's comforted me in the past."

"And it's comforted me, too," seconded Vickery. "Come now, Spayte, you aren't going to fly up and have a fit in the face of Einstein, now are you?"

Spayte furrowed his brow. "All this is interesting. I'll look that passage up. But let's just get back to Thunstone."

"From the sublime to the ridiculous," said Thunstone.

Spayte shook his head impatiently. "Let's get back to you without so many sarcasms. You make everything dark in your room, you say, and that brings you back into what you think is the distant past." Spayte shook his head again. "Could we do that?"

"Maybe not everybody can," said Thunstone. "Maybe it calls for something in a special individual, as with those two schoolmistresses at Versailles."

"Or like you, at Claines," said Vickery. "Or your little witch girl, Constance Bailey you called her. Is she pretty? I do hope so."

"This man Ensley, who's been such a stumbling block to honest researchers," said Spayte. "What does he think about all this? Popping back and forth in time, and so on."

"What he thinks he isn't about to tell," replied Thunstone. "He can irritate you by saying nothing, while all the time he hints that he could say a good deal. He does have one thing he repeats, a reference to ten thousand years ago. Well, I'm going to have dinner with him at his Chimney Pots house tomorrow."

"I hope it's a good dinner," said Vickery.

"Well," said Thunstone, "I've already had a good lunch there. Luncheon, I suppose I should say. But now, gentlemen, I wanted to talk to both of you face to face, give you my report, get your reactions, clarify things by talking. So I'll go catch a bus back to Claines."

"This evening?" said Spayte. "I'd hoped you'd come and stay at my place."

"I'm going to church there tomorrow morning."

"Church?" Vickery almost squeaked, as though that was the strangest thing he had heard from Thunstone. "Look here, I'm coming to Claines with you."

"And I'll do the same, if you'll just give me time to telephone my wife and buy a toothbrush somewhere," said Spayte. "I daresay this Fothergill lady will have lodging for us."

"No, please," said Thunstone. "Don't either of you come."

"Whyever not?" Vickery protested. "All three of us should be there; we could do a lot more than just one."

"I doubt if three could do anything," said Thunstone. "Just I myself have come in for a lot of notice in that little hamlet. Three of us together would be just too rich for the blood of the people. If there's anything to be found out, you can bet it would be squirreled away out of our collective sight."

Spayte frowned at him. "You're going back there alone, then? And whatever are you going to be up to?"

"Frankly, I'm not sure," said Thunstone. "But let me have tonight and tomorrow—Sunday—and Sunday night. They're going to turn the Dream Rock at midnight Sunday, and it's plain that something special is due to happen. If you and Vickery want to visit Claines, come on Monday morning. Ask for me at the Moonraven—that's a good pub, almost as good as this one—or across the street at Mrs. Fothergill's."

"I see," said Vickery. "And what if you aren't there when we come?"

"Then it will be up to you two to find out what's happened to me," Thunstone answered him, "and if you have to do that, get hold of a young constable there by the name of Dymock, and maybe he'll get more police help if he thinks it's needed."

Spayte drained the last drops in his mug. "You talk about this Ensley man of yours and how he can be mysterious. I must say that you've learned the trick from him, learned it very well indeed. Very good, Thunstone, we'll see you sometime Monday morning, I hope."

"I hope," Thunstone echoed him.

They left the Friend at Hand. Spayte headed for his office at the university and Vickery took the underground with Thunstone to see him off at the bus terminal.

The ride to Claines was uneventful. Thunstone occupied his time with jotting down in his notebook some of the things his friends had said at lunch. He pondered the adventure of the Englishwomen at the Trianon gardens as summarized by Vickery, wished he had their book to read, and promised himself to get hold of it as soon as possible.

He got off the bus at the Moonraven parking lot at some time after four o'clock and crossed to Mrs. Fothergill's. He entered his room, and had a sense of familiarity there, as though that had been his living quarters for much longer than three days. The bed had not been disturbed. He pulled back the coverlet and the sheet and saw that the spear lay exactly as he had left it. He took it out and examined it thoroughly.

The haft, he decided, was of ash, and it was as straight as a measuring rod. The point was beautifully chipped to a tapering point, perfectly symmetrical, with toothed edges on both sides of the blade. And the lashing was of stout sinew, of what animal Thunstone could not decide. He hefted the weapon at the balance, wondering how far his unskilled effort could send it.

One thing was certain; it looked new, looked recently and knowledgeably made. Nothing about it suggested a hundred centuries of age. If he showed it to Spayte or Vickery, it would hardly convince them.

Again he made it up in his bed, and went out again.

Mrs. Fothergill met him in the lower hall. She wore a dress the color of daffodils. "So you're back from London after so short a trip; Mr. Hawes said you were going there. On business, I daresay."

"I went to talk to a couple of my friends there," said Thunstone, "and I told them some things about Claines that interested them. They said they might come here for a visit, and I recommended your house to them."

"Thank you so much. Any friends of yours would be entirely welcome here." She smiled again. "By the way, Mr. Thunstone, I thought I'd invite you to take dinner with me after church service tomorrow."

"You're very kind, but I'm invited to Chimney Pots at noon," said Thunstone, rather surprised that one small fact about him was unknown throughout Claines.

"Oh, ah," she said. "If you'll be with Mr. Ensley at noon, might we make it Sunday night supper here, then?"

"Thank you, yes; I'll be with you at supper."

"Just some simple thing, it will be. I'd planned a ham and veal pie; would that suit you?"

"I'll look forward to it," he said. "Sam Weller liked ham and veal pie, as I remember."

"Who? Oh, Sam Weller. In that Pickwick book, isn't he? Yes. Then I'll expect you, Mr. Thunstone."

He bowed and she simpered. He crossed the street again and walked as far as the post office. Dymock stood in front and greeted him with: "Back from London, I see, Mr. Thunstone."

"News of my comings and goings does seem to get around," said Thunstone.

"In a place no larger than Claines, everyone knows all about everyone else, and imagines the rest. And you, sir, an American stranger going here and there, are more or less the topic of the day. London, eh? Great place, that. I hope to be there some day."

"With Scotland Yard," ventured Thunstone.

"Yes, sir, if I'm so fortunate and they decide to want me. By the way, sir, have you seen Connie Bailey about?"

"No, not since I got back from London. Perhaps she's somewhere about Mrs. Fothergill's."

"Not there," said Dymock. "I called around at the back door there not long ago, and she wasn't in."

"Might she be somewhere in the open, perhaps gathering the herbs she uses in her cures and charms?" Thunstone suggested.

"If so, I hope she didn't go up on Sweepside," said Dymock.

"I doubt if she would, considering that Gram Ensley warned her away pretty sharply," said Thunstone.

"I wasn't thinking of Mr. Ensley in particular. I say, see here, Mr. Thunstone," and Dymock swung around to face him. "I think I can flatter myself that you and I have become friends of a sort. I can trust you with what some would call fantastic—ridiculous."

"The fantastic isn't necessarily ridiculous," Thunstone said.

"All right, it's this. We're at a special time of year in Claines, when they shape Old Thunder up, and at midnight on the fourth day of the month—that's your Fourth of July, tomorrow, Sunday midnight—a bunch of men turns the Dream Rock over. The thing can be uncanny for any man of imagination, but this year, this particular year, the time seems more of a time than it should. A little much, if you take my meaning."

"I confess I don't quite," said Thunstone.

"Just more than the usual sense of tenseness," said Dymock. "Sir, in your place I'd be watchful and careful."

"Thanks," said Thunstone. "I will."

He walked along to Ludlam's store and inside. He searched at counters until he found a display of hanks and balls of cord. Looking these over, he found one, of lean but strong plastic, with the label 100 FEET. There was another of the same kind. He took the two to a man behind the counter.

"Do you have any more of these?" he asked. "One more would do me."

"Why, yes, sir, I think we can supply you. Let me look there in the back."

The man went through an inner door and came out with another ball of the plastic cord. "Three in all, you say, sir? Three hundred feet, that will run. Ah, let's see, the price—"

Thunstone paid it and left the store with his three balls of cord in a paper sack.

It was six o'clock, or nearly. Thunstone went to the Moonraven, where Hawes greeted him at the door and Mrs. Hawes from behind the bar. Thunstone asked her for a pint of lager and sat at a table, where the plump, smiling waitress Rosie came to say that the ordinary on Saturday was roast chicken. Thunstone asked her to bring him some, the dark meat if convenient, with whatever vegetables they had that didn't come out of a can. She whipped away with his order.

The place was fairly well filled with customers. At a table across the room sat Porrask. He caught Thunstone's eye and nodded, rather embarrassedly.

The dinner was brought and Thunstone paid for it and ate it, almost without deciding whether it was good or bad. As he was finishing, Constance Bailey came to his table and sat down.

"I thought you'd be here, Mr. Thunstone," she said in her hushed voice.

"Will you have something?" he invited. "Shall I bring you a gin and bitters?"

"No, no thank you. I only want to talk."

"Constable Dymock was looking for you a while ago. He seemed concerned about you."

"Really?" She bowed her head shyly. "He's a good man at his post in life; I hope he keeps his eyes and wits about him tonight and tomorrow. But what I was wondering, you went into town, and I hope you'll let me ask you if you found out anything about—about—"

"Yes," said Thunstone. "I had my attention directed to an interesting case of going back to a former time, and something like an attempt to rationalize it. Apparently some people, maybe only a few people, have the ability to make that trip. People like us, like you and me."

"But why us?" she wondered.

"I don't suppose that's easy to answer. The point is, we've accomplished it. I'm going to try it again when it's dark."

"Not me," she said, her voice trembling. "I'll stay in my room, and I won't turn off my light all night."

"That's just as well. I'll do better alone. Don't worry; I'll keep my weather eye out."

"I wonder," she said, "what would happen if all the lights in Claines were to go out—if a whacking great storm or something put out the electricity and made all dark, everywhere."

"That's interesting to think about," said Thunstone, "and let's hope it doesn't happen. But I'll just darken my own room for the sake of the experience. Now I'll be going."

Back at his room upstairs in Mrs. Fothergill's house, he made various preparations. First he brought the spear out of his bed and laid it across his knees. He took one ball of the plastic cord he had bought, loosened the end of it, and lashed the end tight to the middle of the spear's haft. The other two balls of cord he tucked into the side pockets of his jacket. He found his pencil flashlight and clipped it into his breast pocket. He drew his silver blade from the shank of his cane and hooked the handle on his arm. Finally he sat on the edge of his bed, where he had put himself on the two previous nights. There he waited, with his thoughts for company.

It took a long time for the light to fade, but Thunstone knew how to wait. As dusk followed twilight, he turned on the electric lamp above his bed. He sat silently.

Darkness came to the window and deepened there. The late summer night had come. Thunstone put his hand to his light and turned it off, and the darkness rushed around him, too.

At once he sat on the rocky, lichen-tufted hummock. Again his room was gone from around him. He was in the open, with stars in the sky overhead, with a brisk chilliness in the dark air, with, over yonder, flickering, ruddy points of fire and a distant mutter of sound.

# CHAPTER 11

Again Thunstone examined the spear in his hand, tested the spring of the haft, examined the hard knot with which he had made it fast to the cord. Then he groped to find a crevice in the rock on which he sat, pushed the stone point well into the crevice, and bore down with all his strength. When he was sure that the head of the spear had driven well in and was firmly lodged in the rock, he stood up, holding the ball of cord in his left hand, his sword in his right.

He took a careful step, two steps more, feeling his way with his feet on the dark, tangled turf. As he moved away from the lump of rock which was his sole point of reference, he unrolled the line, loop by loop of it. The sky above his head was strewn with stars in patterns he knew. The air had a chilly bite to it.

Up ahead there, the noise grew greater, seemed to be of voices raised in chorus. There was a definite melody to them. Lights shone at that place, but faint ones, as of several very small fires. The darkness everywhere else was deep, it was oppressive. He peered to see what was yonder, at a distance perhaps like that of Chimney Pots in the Claines he knew.

No, not so much firelight there as he had seemed to see the night before. What light there was picked out human figures, a stirring group of them, as many, perhaps, as twenty. They chanted, or at least a sound like a measured chant came from them. Thunstone kept paying out his cord as he stole along, doing his best to keep it from slackening or tangling. Now the ball had rolled away to its end. He had walked a hundred feet from his rocky hummock. He stood with his blade hung by its crooked handle to one forearm. He took a fresh ball of cord from one of his side pockets, picked an end free and knotted it securely to the end of the cord he had already paid out. Then he moved forward again.

Maybe he was being a fool. Leslie Spayte would call him one, if Spayte should ever come to believe this adventure of his. Yet, Thunstone argued to himself, fools were needed to take the unnecessary chances—the first explorers risking their lives in voyages on unknown seas, the first men to dare to fly into unknown space. And time here became space, that was what Vickery had said, bringing Einstein and Dunne into it.

Standing still for a moment, he gazed to his right at the dimly defined expanse of Sweepside. Upon its surface lay Old Thunder, the tracery of the figure showing palely as though with a light of its own. Constance Bailey had said something about that night before last, about Old Thunder "shining like." Thunstone wondered if the exposed chalk could have a quality of phosphorescence, or if the light of the stars was reflected. He looked at Old Thunder and felt that Old Thunder looked at him.

He advanced again, step by careful step, over grassy ground that was strange, forbidding, under his feet.

The length of that first paid-out stretch of cord must have taken him well away from what, in the time he knew, would be an upper room in Mrs. Fothergill's house. By now he was walking over grass-tufted ground, where the neighboring cottages would stand someday —where they already stood, in that other extension of time. How could he remember those cottages when, here in this now, they had not yet been built? The matter took thinking about, and did he have time to think? Time here, in this here, this now? He doubted it. He walked on, sliding his feet to be sure of where they held to the ground.

It took him almost no time at all to reach the end of his second hundred feet of cord. He spliced on the third ball, and looked back the way he had come. Nothing showed there in the heavy night. No sign of where his journey had begun, or of the place to which he must return to be safe again.

More slowly he resumed his approach toward the fires and the people, the creatures that moved and chanted there. His three hundred feet of line would never bring him close, but he could see much more clearly now. The people danced, he thought, danced naked. From the point he had reached, he could tell which dancers were male, which female, except for one figure. That one stood motionless in the midst of the dancers, stood head and shoulders above them. It looked blotched or dappled. Thunstone thought it had horns, perhaps a headdress of horns.

As he stood and strained his eyes to see, feet trampled nearer at hand. Shapes came toward him, three of them. They moved fast, almost at a run.

It had been that way the night before. Perhaps these primitive celebrants kept outlying sentinels, to guard whatever ritual was performed there in the glow of the fires. Thunstone watched them as they approached him purposefully. He tucked the cord into his waistband and shifted the blade to his right hand. He held it saber fashion, fingers clasped around the hilt, thumb lying snug at the top. As the three closed in upon him, he advanced his silver point.

"Good evening," he said.

One of the trio sprang ahead of its companions. It was a stocky figure in some sort of fur tunic, with a great shock of hair to crown its head. One hand flung up an ax or perhaps a stone-headed club, ready to deal a sweeping downward blow. Thunstone chose the exact second to slide his right foot forward and extend his arm in a lunge, and the oncoming body spitted itself on his blade. He heard a strangled cry and saw the thing go stumbling down in the darkness. As it sank, he cleared his weapon and fell on guard to face the others.

They had pressed so close together in their charge that their companion's falling body jostled them, drove them staggering apart. They paused, for only a breath's space. Then the one to Thunstone's left emitted a wordless roar and thrust with a spear held in both hands.

Thunstone slapped the weapon aside with his left forearm. As the spear drove past him, he extended his own point toward the center of an oncoming body clad in some sort of shaggy hide. He felt it go home, felt it grate on a rib as it sank deep into the chest. Then another of his assailants was down, and the third fell away, retreated half a dozen paces.

"You're biting off more than you can chew," Thunstone addressed him and took time to try to see this survivor.

The starlight gave him some notion of a rangy shape, bare-armed, bare-legged, with a rude garment covering the chest and loins. That garment was made of a pelt, roughly fitted like the clothes of the others, possibly from some sort of heavy-haired bull, possibly even from a bear. The feet seemed to wear rude buskins, also shaggy and extending halfway up to the knee. Staring eyes twinkled, eyes that in a better light might show pale and icy. The face below them had a frill of beard, not greatly different from that of Albert Porrask. One hand lifted a spear, but the spear wavered indecisively.

All this Thunstone saw in an instant.

"Afraid, are you?" Thunstone taunted. "Then you have a grain of sense, after all. Gram Ensley and I were agreeing that your generation wasn't altogether senseless."

Again he gathered his cord in his left hand, sword still raised and ready. He stole forward, right foot sliding first, then the left coming up behind, then the right foot again, the fencer's half-shuffling advance. The other stayed no longer. He whipped around and ran swiftly, at the same time shouting at the top of his lungs. He was using words; he had language of a sort.

Another loud shout answered from the group around the fire, and by the light there Thunstone could see half a dozen naked figures pull away and start toward him.

He, too, waited no longer, but turned back the way he had come. He followed his cord, hand after hand, along its slim length. Behind him rose a chorus of voices, with menace in them. He quickened his pace as much as he could. The reinforcing group was after him, no doubt about that. He thought for a moment of turning to face whatever attack might come; he wanted to turn and face it, but knew that that would be utter rashness and bravado. He continued his retreat as fast as he could run the line through his hands.

The noise behind him grew ever louder. Voices bellowed in hot fury, feet stamped. They saw him, they were angry, and, as he guessed, they were gaining. But then, thank God, he was at his rocky hummock, where the spear stood upright.

At last he took time for a glance back. On the night grass several of the group had stopped, bent down to look at something, undoubtedly at the bodies of the two Thunstone had stabbed and killed. The others ran toward him. He yanked the spear from its lodgment in the split rock, tucked it under his arm with his blade, and from his pocket snatched the pencil flashlight. He gazed at his pursuers, close at hand, weapons at the ready.

Then he touched the switch, and glow sprang up to show him the quiet interior of his room at Mrs. Fothergill's, the desk and the chairs, with the bed close to where he stood.

At once he turned on the light above the bed and sat down in its comforting glow. He examined his long, lean blade of silver. It ran blood almost to the hilt, wet and gleaming darkly red, the blood of the Stone Age.

He sighed deeply. From time to time in his adventures, Thunstone had killed fellow creatures. It had always been for dire necessity, but not once had he ever rejoiced in it. He fumbled out his handkerchief and carefully wiped the blade shinily clean. He studied the red stains on the handkerchief. Then he folded it carefully. Quite possibly some medical man—Jules de Grandin for one—would be interested in making chemical tests of the blood of a man who had died in England's far-off times.

He wrapped the folded handkerchief in a sheet of paper and stowed it in an inner pocket of his suitcase. He leaned the spear against the wall and restored his silver sword blade to the shank of its cane. For a moment he had the impulse to turn off the light above the bed, to plunge the room into darkness and plunge himself back into that ancient age where he had adventured perilously, where he had struck down two men of that stone-chipping time. Would the others be gathered at the hummock by now, at the spot where he must have vanished before their eyes?

The temptation was strong, but Thunstone brushed it away. It was his duty to be as safe as possible, to make a record, to come to a solution of all the enigmas which clung darkly around Claines.

Again he had things to write. Sitting at the desk, he filled page after page with the account of his night's experience and his reactions to it. He referred to the spear he had captured and told where the bloody handkerchief could be found in his suitcase. Finally he folded the written pages into an envelope, and upon it he wrote:

In case of the disappearance or disability of
JOHN THUNSTONE
deliver this into the hands of
LESLIE SPAYTE OR PHILO VICKERY
who will be in Claines on Monday morning, July 5

He tilted the envelope against the back of the desk, and felt better that it was there.

Then he took off his clothes, put on his robe, and sought the bathroom to take his nightly shower. As he soaped his brawny left forearm, he was aware of a slight scrape on the skin. He rinsed it off and studied it. That was where he had fended off the thrust of a spear of the Rough Stone Age. There, late in this twentieth century, was his souvenir of an encounter with an adversary of a century too long ago to date surely, an adversary who could have been his own ancestor. He had killed that adversary, had dealt him a mortal wound. Again he felt unhappy because that had been necessary. And he wondered what the man's companions could think about someone, a stranger, bobbing in and out of their awareness to strike and kill.

Back in his room, he put on pajamas and stretched out on the bed. As before, he left on the light. Hands behind his head, he thought and thought.

Here he lay under the protection of the electric light, late in his own twentieth century. Switch off the light, and he would instantly go back yet again to that other remote century. Did Gram Ensley mean something about that time when he kept talking about ten thousand years ago? If Thunstone turned out his light now and returned to the lichened hummock he had begun to know, he might have company close at hand, unfriendly company armed with sharp stone weapons. He had told Constance Bailey that he did not fear death, and he did not fear it, but he felt no zest for courting it just now. Very likely he would have ample chances for courting it later.

He went to sleep at last, and slept soundly. His dreams were not of bleak night landscapes and dancers in firelight, but of pleasant moments in faraway cities. He thought that he sat at a table, sipping wine and talking to someone he knew, someone with fair hair and rosy cheeks, who smiled and smiled her happiness to be with him.

Waking in the morning, he shaved as usual and went back to his room to dress as conventionally as possible for a Sunday visit to church. He put on dark trousers instead of the checked ones he had been wearing, a white shirt and a soberly patterned necktie and his dark jacket. Downstairs, Mrs. Fothergill welcomed him radiantly and introduced him to three other guests, two women and a man, and they went in to sit down to breakfast.

"This is the day you Americans celebrate, Mr. Thunstone," said Mrs. Fothergill, pouring coffee. "The Fourth of July, your Independence Day. We British rejoice with you. It's too bad that we aren't the same nation now."

"Amen," said one of the ladies. "You say you'll be at church today. We drove in past that church on our way from London. Noticed it. It's a small church, isn't it?"

Mrs. Fothergill obliged with some talk about St. Jude's, how old it was, and how it was really only part of a larger parish at Gerrinsford. She amplified with talk about David Gates the curate and his almost frantic activity on behalf of St. Jude's. "But not a great many attend services," she said. "Today, this morning, I don't expect attendance to be out of the twenty-five or thirty."

"More, then, at your church here than at our home place," said the other lady, buttering toast.

"Will Mr. Ensley come to church today?" Thunstone asked Mrs. Fothergill.

"If he does that, I'll wonder at it," she said. "He attends very little, though they do say he makes contributions. Mr. Ensley is a more or less secret man, withdrawn. Today you'll be entertained by him the second time since you came here—first time was on the Thursday, right?"

"Friday," said Thunstone.

"Not many get inside Chimney Pots twice in the year."

Breakfast over, Thunstone strolled outside. The morning was

bright, warm, with sunshine. He gazed up at Old Thunder on Sweepside. The figure looked more misshapen than before, and Thunstone wondered if it had been relined in any way. A voice spoke beside him. It was Constance Bailey.

"What is it, Mr. Thunstone? You're having a look at Old Thunder."

"Yes," he said. "Have you noticed that, in that other place you and I can go when it's dark, Old Thunder glows?"

"I don't think I've noticed," she confessed. "I'm always too afraid to notice any much of things."

"But it's not Old Thunder I'm thinking about," he told her. "I'm thinking about how the people of Claines turn the Dream Rock every year, always at midnight."

"Always at midnight," she repeated. "The witching hour, somebody said."

"That was Shakespeare," said Thunstone. "And once I heard somebody explain midnight as the logical time for strange, evil things to happen. I think I can quote what he said exactly, it made a big impression on me." He paused, remembering. Then: " 'It's exactly midway between sunset and sunrise. Allows the supernatural force to split the dark hours halfway—half for the summoning of courage and strength to come forth, half to do whatever is in hand to do.' "

Constance Bailey stared at him, impressed. "I say, I never thought of the thing like that, but it's the solemn truth. Whoever told that to you?"

"His name was Rowley Thorne. He was an enemy of mine."

"Was?" she said after him. "Was? You mean, he's dead?"

"I earnestly hope so," Thunstone said. Still he gazed up the slope toward Old Thunder. "Tell me," he said, "does that figure seem to move?"

"It shimmers," she said. "Dances, you might say. Maybe the sun on it makes it happen like that in my eyes."

"Maybe," he said. "How did you rest last night?"

"Oh, all very well, considering," she replied. "Slept with my light on. I fancy Mrs. Fothergill wouldn't like my light burning, but I did leave it. Otherwise—" She shuddered. "Otherwise I'd have been out there, out where you and I know. If I may ask, did you rest well too?"

"After I got back," he said. "I ventured back into that place and time."

"Ow," and she shuddered again. "What happened?"

"Several interesting things. I'm still speculating on them."

He turned his back on Sweepside and watched traffic on Trail Street. The other overnight guests came out of the house, got into a little car that surprisingly held them all and their luggage too, and went driving away toward the east. As they went, they chattered about how excited they would be at the place for which they were bound. Thunstone speculated that excitement enough would involve Claines when the Dream Rock was turned at midnight.

Dream Rock, he said to himself. What had the Dream Rock once been, what had it represented? What relationship was there between the Dream Rock and Old Thunder? Again he turned and gazed up at the outline in the chalk. It seemed to dance again, shimmer again, as when he and Constance Bailey had stood looking. That couldn't be natural. But it shimmered and danced, natural or not. Thunstone wondered what sort of danger he had come to in Claines.

He thought yet again about death and the fear of it, and the times he had come close to death. There had been Rowley Thorne whose name he had mentioned to Constance Bailey, Rowley Thorne who had known so much about the night side of nature but had not known as much as he had flattered himself. There had been those strange people the Shonokins, sure of their title to the American continent, menacing but not undefeatable. And once or twice a vampire, and once or twice a werewolf. Here in Claines, what threatened? For something threatened. Nobody seemed to know what, except perhaps Gram Ensley. And he would be taking dinner today with Gram Ensley, at that huge old house called Chimney Pots.

He looked at his watch. It was well past nine. He went back inside. Mrs. Fothergill beamed at him through the door to her little room that did duty for parlor and office.

"When will church services be?" he asked her.

"Why, at eleven, of course," she replied. "I'll leave here at about half past ten. Will you walk there with me?"

"It will be a pleasure," he said.

"Yes," she agreed. "A pleasure, Mr. Thunstone."

He went up to his room. There, he carefully filled a pipe with tobacco, kinnikinnick, and the shredded bark of red willow. He sat and kindled the pipe and gazed into the rising cloud of blue smoke. That, Long Spear had told him, was one way to see visions of what might come. Such visions would be a welcome change. Just then, Thunstone felt he had had quite enough of visions of the remote past.

The smoke rose in a slaty puff, another puff, another. It seemed to spread out like a fabric. Thunstone gazed into it, trying to see something. If Long Spear could see things in smoke, why not Thunstone? He gazed. He stared.

And saw something, faint, puzzling. He kept his eyes fixed, hoping it would clear. It cleared, a little. He sensed, rather than saw, what was there.

At first he thought that a great, grotesque animal was moving past in front of his eyes. It looked like a distorted dream figure of a dark bull. But though it moved, somehow it seemed static. No movement of the feet. Then he saw what the thing was—a picture of some kind, bizarre but at the same time workmanlike, a true picture of a bull. And it did not move. He moved; he was going past it.

Abruptly the sense of it faded before his eyes. He saw something else. It seemed to be a lattice like tracery of lines, and the figure of a man was there against it. He was only a smudgy outline, somebody of powerful build, his hands raised upon the lattice.

As Thunstone looked and wondered, the picture dimmed. The smoke was dissolving into the air; it took the picture with it.

His pipe had gone out. He reached into his pocket for a packet of matches, but did not strike one to rekindle the mixture of herbs and tobacco in the pipe. If Long Spear had been present, Thunstone might have done it. Long Spear was not only a chief of his people, he was a medicine man, could make strong magic. He would be a help here, would interpret. Thunstone wished for him but, without him, decided to evoke no more visions.

A glance at his watch told him that it was nearly half past ten. He rose, looked in the mirror to straighten his necktie, and went downstairs.

Mrs. Fothergill met him in the hall. She had changed into a summer suit of pearly gray, and upon her mass of hair rode one of the flattest hats he had ever seen. In one hand she carried a black prayer book, red-edged.

"Oh, ah," she said. "Are you ready to go to church, then?"

"If you are," he said.

# CHAPTER 12

Side by side they crossed Trail Street, just then strung with traffic. Thunstone took Mrs. Fothergill's arm as though to guide her, and she seemed almost to cuddle against him. On the far side of the street, at the parking space in front of the Moonraven, Hawes the proprietor stood and watched them come toward him.

"It's a fine, fair Sunday," he greeted them. "Good morning to you, Mrs. Fothergill, and good morning to you, Mr. Thunstone. You're for church, I daresay."

"That's right, Mr. Hawes," said Thunstone. "The curate, Mr. Gates, seems especially to want me there."

"I must stay here and open at noon," said Hawes. "I'd like to come, but Mrs. Hawes has to be there at the organ, and we can't both be gone from duty at once. I was at church for early prayer already today."

They continued along the sidewalk. A pudgy woman greeted them. Thunstone recognized her as the postmistress who had sold him stamps.

"Mrs. Fothergill," she said, "and—eh—"

"This is Mr. Thunstone," Mrs. Fothergill told her. "We're on our way to church."

"Ow, Mr. Thunstone," said the postmistress. "Church. Yes indeed."

They walked along. "She'll come to church now, even if she hadn't meant to," said Mrs. Fothergill.

"Why should she change her mind and come?" Thunstone asked. "What's on her mind?"

"For one thing," said Mrs. Fothergill coyly, "she thinks we make a very handsome couple; that's plain enough. Possibly you think the same."

"You're very handsome, anyway," Thunstone let himself say.

"Oh, Mr. Thunstone."

They passed the Waggoner pub, its door closed. Opposite, Chimney Pots looked closed, too, no human motion there.

"Will Mr. Ensley come to church?" asked Thunstone again.

"He attends very rarely. His servants come. Yonder comes one, now, that Hob Sayle person."

As she spoke, Hob Sayle came tramping around the side of the house. He wore a black suit and he made purposefully toward the church.

"But not Mrs. Sayle today," said Mrs. Fothergill. "She'll be busy with the dinner that's to be served you."

She did not sound happy about that. Thunstone changed the subject.

"Quite a few people seem to be afoot this morning," he commented.

"On their way to church, I fancy. The word's gone around that Mr. Gates will have something quite special in the way of a sermon."

"Yes," said Thunstone, "he hinted as much to me."

They approached the church. People were going in at the door. Two or three others lingered outside, talking. They looked at Thunstone and Mrs. Fothergill, but none of them spoke. Thunstone escorted her inside.

The interior of St. Jude's was, not surprisingly, a relatively small auditorium, with walls of a dull brown paneling. Two windows at the front had stained glass. One represented the parable of the sower going forth sowing, with, in gilded letters, the message IN MEMORY OF NATHAN JACKSON MORRISON. The other was older and quainter. It portrayed a haloed figure with draped gown and long beard. Possibly it was meant to represent St. Jude himself. Other windows at the two sides were of plain glass.

Pews on either side of the aisle looked solid, old, unshowy. They had dim cushions. People already sat in the rear pews, avoiding the front ones as usual in a church. Up at the far end was an altar with vases of flowers upon it, and candles in sconces. Forward of the altar, to right and left, stood small lecterns, and, centered midway between them, the pulpit. There did not seem to be ushers.

As Thunstone showed Mrs. Fothergill into a pew and sat down beside her, a mutter of music rose. That was from a small electric organ to one side, where an unimaginative choir loft had been built. The organist was Mrs. Hawes in a flowered hat, playing carefully and not badly.

More worn old cushions lay on the floor in front of the pew, and Thunstone and Mrs. Fothergill knelt in the traditional moment of prayer, then slid back and sat. The pews filled up. They seemed even crowded. Stealthy whispers crept in the air. Then David Gates entered at a rear door, in cassock and alb, carrying in his massive hands a long rod furnished with a length of lighted wicking. He crossed in front of the altar, noticing it as he did so, and lighted the candles on that side. He crossed back, with another bow to notice the altar, and lighted the others. Then he went out through the rear door again.

"Mr. Gates would be so happy if he could get acolytes to do that sort of thing for him," Mrs. Fothergill whispered to Thunstone.

The music of the little organ rose, began to be a hymn. At the church door behind the pews, voices were singing. A procession of sorts moved along the aisle.

At the front, in the crucifer's place, paced Hob Sayle, the manservant of Gram Ensley, bearing the processional cross like a banner. He wore a white cotta and stepped his way proudly. Behind him moved two men, then two women, also in cottas and carrying open hymnbooks and singing. One of the women was Rosie, the plump waitress. She seemed to have a good soprano voice. They marched to the altar, where Sayle planted the cross in its socket. Then they entered the choir loft. Sayle went with them and stood there, joining in the hymn.

At the rear of the formation had marched Gates, gigantic seeming now that he wore an ornamented chasuble over his alb and cassock and had draped his neck with a stole. He stopped before the altar, knelt for a moment, then rose and came to the pulpit, facing the listeners. His face looked bigger and broader than ever, and tense to boot.

The service went forward on the traditionally prescribed lines. Gates read the collect for the Third Sunday after Trinity, a humble and trusting appeal enough. When it came to reading the proper epistle, which is from the first chapter of St. Peter, he began quietly enough, though rather grimly. But his voice rose suddenly, even fiercely, as he read out:

Be sober, be vigilant; because your adversary the devil, as a roaring lion, walketh about, seeking whom he may devour.

Similarly, he began quietly as he read the Gospel for the Third Sunday after Trinity, from the Gospel of St. Luke. But he raised his voice significantly when he came to the passage:

I say unto you, that likewise joy shall be in heaven over one sinner that repenteth, more than over ninety and nine just persons, which need no repentance.

From step to step the service proceeded. At last, David Gates announced several church activities, a collection for foreign missions, a meeting of church ladies for a community project, and so on. After that, it was time for the sermon.

Gates drew himself up at the pulpit and stood impressively tall. His attitude was more that of a prosecuting attorney than of a minister of the Gospel. He gazed to this side and that, his eyes burning palely as they raked the congregation.

"For this day I have chosen a text singularly appropriate," he declared. "It will be familiar to all of you. It is to be found in the twentieth chapter of the Book of Exodus, the second verse. It is also easily to be found in our Book of Common Prayer, the first of the Ten Commandments, and the most important among them all. In the Scriptures it reads, 'Thou shalt have no other gods before me.' "

He squared his broad shoulders and looked at them again, pew after pew of them, as though to note the effect of his words.

"That is the command of God our Father," he said, "spoken to Moses at the top of Mount Sinai, to be cut by him on the tables of stone. It disavows, it forbids, the turning after false gods to worship them. Now, today is the Third Sunday after Trinity, and the fourth day of July. And the fourth day of July also happens to be the day of the year on which, in this our community of Claines, a bizarre and infamous heathen ceremony is traditionally accomplished at the hour of midnight."

His voice shook, as though he strove to master a fury within himself. "I refer," he said, "to the annual turning over of what is called the Dream Rock that lies out there at the edge of the street in front of this church, this holy church."

He clamped his meaty hands on the sides of the pulpit and leaned powerfully forward above it. The folds of the chasuble stirred upon him. Fiercely he gazed. It was as though he menaced his listeners.

"Against this pagan ceremony I shall preach this morning. I promise you that my sermon will not be a long one, nor shall I search out elegant, elaborate words and phrases. I shall strive to make it simple and forthright; because I want it to be well understood by all of you. And if you care to repeat what I say to others who are not with us here this morning, why, so much the better."

Another pause, as though to gather himself for his next words. All listened raptly. Some leaned forward in their pews. Hob Sayle sat stiffly in his chair in the choir loft. He gaped, he stared. He seemed to hold his breath.

"Think, my people," burst out Gates. "Why are they here so close together, St. Jude's little church and that strange, uncouth menhir called the Dream Rock? I can assure you that this is no accident, no fortuity. How long ago they built the first church of St. Jude's here, there can be no sure saying, but it was long, long ago, centuries ago. It was built here under a classic missionary policy."

Another breathing space.

"Our first ancestors, here and elsewhere in Britain, were pagans, of course," Gates went on. "For untold centuries, for centuries almost past counting, they worshipped false gods, sacrificed to them—sacrificed wild beasts and tame, sometimes even their unfortunate fellow men. The Roman legions came and brought in their own culture and their own pantheon, their string of Latin deities from Jupiter on

down, and worshipped them far and near until the Roman Empire
was enlightened by Christian faith. But that faith suffered in turn in
Britain, was put down by the conquering invasion of the Angles and
Saxons. They followed their own barbarous heathen worship of
Wotan and Thor and other Teutonic gods, until Christianity was
returned to our land by Saint Augustine."

Gates warmed to the old story of missionary strategy and success,
telling the oft-told tale of how Pope Gregory the First—Gregorius,
Gates called him, apparently forgetting his promise to stick to plain
language—showed a somewhat sophisticated tact toward the Saxon
pagans. Taking up a sheet of paper, Gates read a translation of
Gregory's instructions:

> If these temples are well built, it is requisite that they be
> converted from the worship of devils to the service of the true
> God; that the nation, seeing that their temples are not de-
> stroyed, may remove error from their hearts and knowing and
> adoring the true God may the more frequently resort to places to
> which they have been accustomed.

Philo Vickery had mentioned that policy, Thunstone remembered
as he listened.

Gates finished reading, and fairly flung the paper down on the
pulpit. His broad palm slapped the wood resoundingly.

"There, my people," he said, "a missionary work was well begun
here in Britain. The Saxons proved adaptable, reasonable. Their very
kings gladly accepted the true faith. Their ancient places of worship
were purified with holy water and prayer and those places became
Christian churches. Why?" His voice rose suddenly. "The older
cathedral at Salisbury stood on the site of just such a place of pagan
worship. And it was so with many, many others. Let me read to you
from John Milton's beautiful work, 'On the Morning of Christ's
Nativity.' "

He then read extensively from that poem. He chose verses which
described the banishment of the gods of Greece and Rome, of Philis-
tia, Phoenicia, and Egypt. Plainly he enjoyed the reading, and he
smiled as he finished.

"The uncouth festivals of those barbarians also were adopted and adapted by the church and its communicants," he said. "Beltane became our happy May Day, when country folk dance around the pole and choose their king and queen of the May. Halloween, our eve of All Hallows, falls on the ancient date of Saunhaim, the Celtic festival for the dead. The old Midsummer Day, when once Druids sacrificed human victims, is now Saint John's. And so on. And, as I have said, all throughout this land churches rose on the sites, the very graves, of heathen rites and worship. More than a hundred such churches can be pointed out, in England and Ireland and Scotland and Wales, including our church of St. Jude's."

He returned to citations from the Bible. He dwelt with relish upon the story of how Elijah contended with the priests of Baal on Mount Carmel; of Elijah's sneering mockery of Baal's priests when they could not pray fire down upon their sacrifice, Elijah's triumph when his appeal to Yahweh kindled his own altar, and the massacre of the unsuccessful priests afterward.

"Thus have the true and false faiths contended, side by side, through time," he summed up impressively. "Now need we stir from here to see the evidence at first hand?"

He pointed a big forefinger, and the wide sleeve fluttered on his arm like a wing.

"Yes, my people, out there!" he fairly roared. "Out at the edge of our own church's yard, our own holy ground, lies the relic of a false belief that has not yet died! Though Saint Augustine and his fellow missionaries hoped and strove, that thing exists and its ritual is observed in Claines, even upon this day! You know what I mean. I mean the Dream Rock, and the dreams it gives are dreams of the pit below the very floor of hell itself!"

He gestured downward as he spoke, as though to indicate to his hearers where the floor of hell was. A sigh went up from those who listened. They hung upon the words he gave them.

"For how many years, for how many lifetimes, has the Dream Rock been turned at this midnight?" he flung out at them. "And what does it signify, portend, this annual turning? My people, I've looked into the most ancient records I could find. And I have not found a year in those records when the turning is not noted as taking place. At midnight—the witching time of night when, says Shakespeare, churchyards yawn and hell itself breathes out contagion to this world. That's always the hour when the Dream Rock is turned over in its place, by those who think they have good reasons for the turning."

Gates flourished both his big hands. "Reasons?" he said again. "What might those reasons be, pray? I wonder if anyone here present, or away from here at home in Claines, can give plain reasons. The custom's been passed on through time, from grandfather to father to son. I would feel no surprise to learn that these turners of the Dream Rock are not sure themselves why they do that turning. No! They turn the thing because it has always been turned, isn't that so?"

He clenched his hands. They made fists as rugged as cobbles.

"Oh yes," he said, "I've had advice on this matter, well-meant advice from high places, about letting ancient traditions alone, letting ancient traditions take their course, go on as they have gone so long. And, as you know if you've been out at midnight of a fourth of July to watch the turning of that triply cursed rock, you know that never yet have I attended. But—"

One fist raised itself on high.

"I'll be out there this midnight," he promised at the top of his lungs. "I'll be present to forbid that turning, forbid it as it is my duty —my duty as a clergyman, a man of God. And here and now, let me give warning. I am a strong man of God. I have muscles in these arms. God has given me these thews and sinews. He has found it good that I have exercised them, schooled them. I can use them in the service of the right and the true. And—"

Yet another fearsome sweep of his blazing eyes.

"If there are those out tonight who, in spite of my warning, try to turn the Dream Rock, I shall oppose them; I shall resist them! Let my vow to do that go forth in Claines, too!"

With that he fell silent, and the church, too, was silent. He leaned heavily on the pulpit, as though the vigor of his speaking had wearied him. He breathed deeply, drawing in great panting lungfuls of air. Thunstone saw sweat on his brow beneath the tossed fair hair.

When he spoke again, it was quietly, almost tonelessly, to announce the offertory:

"To do good, and to distribute, forget not; for with such sacrifices God is well pleased."

Mrs. Hawes struck a chord on her organ and began to play a selection that Thunstone did not know. Two men, dressed in suits of consciously decent drab cloth, came forward to take gray plates and return along the aisle, passing the plates along each pew in turn. Thunstone put a five pound note in the plate, noticing as he did so that the plate was of dull pewter with a crude but interesting antique design around its edge. Such a piece, he reflected, was undoubtedly old and rare; a collector would pay a big price for it. When the collection was finished, the two men stood at the head of the aisle and waited.

Rosie sang a solo then, and it was a hymn that Thunstone had always liked, "There is a Green Hill Far Away." Her voice was pleasant, tuneful. When she was done, the men fetched the plates forward and Gates recognized the offerings with some words of prayer and placed them on the altar.

He then pronounced the benediction. The choir began another hymn, while Gates moved almost hurriedly away toward a rear door. The choir proceeded up the aisle and away, and when the hymn was finished all rose and moved to depart.

Mrs. Fothergill spoke to several acquaintances on the way out, but stayed close to Thunstone, a hand on his arm. Outside the front door, Gates stood, shaking hands with men and women and speaking to them. Mrs. Fothergill made a fluttery occasion of taking his hand.

"What an eloquent sermon, Father Gates," she bubbled, "but it was a bit frightening, too."

"So I meant it to be, Mrs. Fothergill," he assured her readily. "Mr. Thunstone, you kept your promise to attend services."

"I do my best to keep all my promises," said Thunstone. "Now, we're to understand that you'll be present beside the Dream Rock at midnight. I want to be present, too. That's why I came to Claines in the first place."

"And if I should need your help, Mr. Thunstone? Your physical help?"

"If you need it, I'll give it as well as I can."

"Thank you, thank you."

At least a dozen men and women stood listening. They stared at Gates, at Thunstone, two big men who were promising to be there at midnight. Hob Sayle was one who watched and listened. After a moment, he strolled to where the Dream Rock lay and gazed thoughtfully down at it.

Gates turned away to speak to another couple. Thunstone and Mrs. Fothergill walked together along Trail Street.

# CHAPTER 13

Others who walked on Trail Street met Mrs. Fothergill and Thunstone and spoke to them. Mrs. Fothergill glowed as she exchanged words of greeting. Plainly she was glad to be seen walking with Thunstone. They had almost reached her doorstep when she first mentioned the sermon Gates had delivered.

"Those were powerful words," she said. "Fighting words, I should call them."

"He means to stop the turning of the Dream Rock tonight, that's plain," said Thunstone.

"And sounded ready to fight," Mrs. Fothergill went on. "With his fists, I mean."

"I judge that he can do that," said Thunstone. "He told me that he had boxed for his university, boxed heavyweight."

"I don't know anything about boxing," confessed Mrs. Fothergill, "but I should fancy that he would be quite good. And you told him you'd help him. Can you box, Mr. Thunstone?"

"I've done a little of that in my time."

They mounted the front steps and went into the hall. "Now," she said, "you'll be for dinner with Mr. Ensley. Mightn't I offer you a glass of something before you go?"

"Thank you, but Mr. Ensley will have drinks, and I'm no heavy drinker."

"Oh, to be sure. I quite understand. Maybe later this evening, then, before our little supper tonight." She smiled, as though thoughts of supper pleased her. "Don't eat too great a dinner; leave some room for the ham and veal pie."

"I'll leave room," he promised.

"And when you come back, you can tell me something about Chimney Pots." Her smile became conspiratorial. "About who it is who stays there with Mr. Ensley, that woman of mystery."

"Doesn't anybody know who she is?" he asked.

"No." Mrs. Fothergill shook her head. "He brought her here in his car, oh about five months ago. All anybody saw of her was her rich fur coat. And once or twice, there have been glimpses of her, here and there among the trees behind the house."

"Then she doesn't come out into the village, to the shops or anywhere?"

"Not she. And Mr. Ensley doesn't speak of her, and nobody here would think of asking him, wouldn't ever dream. Nobody knows a thing of her, not even her name."

"I know that she plays the piano and paints pictures," said Thunstone. "But I haven't met her."

"Well, if you should meet her today, bring back a report, then. I'm so curious."

Up in his room, Thunstone communed with his pipe. He promised himself an interesting visit to St. Jude's when the Dream Rock was turned at midnight, and permitted himself to wonder if David Gates, with his sturdy determination and formidable fists, might not be able to prevent that turning. In any case, Thunstone would be there to find out.

He finished smoking his pipe, tapped it out, and slid it into the side pocket of his jacket, along with the pouch that held the mixture of herbs and tobacco. As he stowed the things away, he noticed that his small flashlight was still clipped in his breast pocket. He left it there, picked up his sword cane, and went out.

He strolled slowly along Trail Street. A number of people were out in the bright Sunday air. Fully half a dozen of these spoke to Thunstone, calling him by name. It was as though he were a well-known, well-liked resident of Claines, where actually he had been for less than three full days. His watch told him that it was almost exactly half-past one when he came opposite Chimney Pots. He crossed over, mounted the wide, low porch and swung the brass knocker on the massive door. He waited. Inside, the piano made music.

Hob Sayle opened the door to him, wearing a white linen jacket. "Mr. Thunstone," he said. "Please come in, sir. Mr. Ensley is expecting you."

"Yes, Mr. Thunstone, come in." That was Ensley, walking toward him in the entry hall, with the music of the piano behind him. Bach, Thunstone recognized at once, a two-part invention. Ensley was dressed in a tawny jacket and slacks, and in his lapel he wore a tiny pink flower.

"Come in, come in," he invited again, taking Thunstone's hand and shaking it.

Thunstone leaned his cane against the stand of armor. He went with Ensley into the drawing room he remembered from his previous visit. The music was there.

A young woman sat at the piano. Thunstone's first impression was of pallor, pale hair, pale face, a sort of glow like a night-blooming flower. She stopped playing and rose to her feet. She was tall and seemed taller for the high-heeled shoes she wore. Her dress was of soft black fabric and it clung close to her proud, slim figure. A rope of pearls hung around her neck and down upon the soft curve of her bosom.

"Gonda," Ensley addressed her, "this is Mr. Thunstone. I've mentioned him to you."

"How do you do," she said in a sweet, deep voice. She had an oval face, creamy-skinned, with a short, pink mouth and eyes somewhat aslant and as blue as the sea on a cloudy day. Her short hair, almost fleecily curly, was so blond as to be almost ashen. She was not an albino, but it took a second look to make sure of that. Thunstone had never seen so light a complexion.

"How do you do, Miss Gonda," said Thunstone, taking the long, slim hand she held out to him.

"Please," she said softly, "my name is Gonda, only Gonda. All the name I use." She spoke with the smallest touch of an accent.

"Gonda is Norse," contributed Ensley. "She is greatly talented in various fields. You have heard her play, and these paintings on the front wall are hers. But sit down and talk for a moment, and won't you have a trifle of sherry before we eat?"

Thunstone and Gonda sat in armchairs. Ensley went to the sideboard and poured from a tall bottle into stemmed glasses. He offered these, sat down himself, and lifted his own glass. "Cheers," he said hospitably.

It was an excellent sherry. Thunstone sipped appreciatively, and looked at the paintings Ensley had indicated on the front wall, paintings he had not had time to study on his previous visit.

The largest of them was done rather somberly in dark oils, brown and gray-blue and gray-black, with only touches of brightness in two places. It seemed to be a night scene, with a pale disc of a moon in the gloomy sky and a tag of orange firelight on the ground below. Around the fire crowded figures, darker than the darkness, barely touched by the glow of the fire. To Thunstone, they looked like something he had seen.

"How did you come to paint that, Gonda?" he asked.

"It was what you might call a vision," she replied. "More or less."

"And a highly interesting vision it is, wouldn't you say?" asked Ensley from where he sat. "Don't you have visions, Mr. Thunstone?"

"Don't all human creatures have visions?" asked Thunstone in turn. "And don't the visions become realities sometimes?"

"I can believe that," said Gonda, her slim white hand poising her sherry glass, while a jewel sparkled on her ring.

"I'm interested in what both of you might say about visions," said Ensley. "Mr. Thunstone, you and I have touched on the subject before this. We recognized the possibility that Claines is particularly rich in the stuff of visions."

"I remember," nodded Thunstone. "And you spoke of times ten thousand years ago, in the Old Stone Age."

"Ten thousand years ago is an even hundred centuries," said Ensley. "Claines has been here that long, in some sort of established community. My finds of artifacts, of the traces of old habitations, prove as much."

"And Chimney Pots?" asked Thunstone.

"Hardly as old as all that." Ensley smiled. "Stone Age homebuilders had far less elaborate notions of architecture. But

Chimney Pots has been recognizable, name and all, for several centuries at least."

"It has a true feeling of antiquity," offered Gonda.

"Of course, it has gone through changes and alterations," Ensley went on. "But it stands, I feel certain, where once a Stone Age habitation stood."

"Indeed?" said Thunstone.

"After dinner, perhaps, I can show you some evidence of that. Historically, I mean in times of written history, Chimney Pots was some sort of fortress. During the Wars of the Roses, that is, and again during the Civil War—I'm speaking of our Civil War, Mr. Thunstone, not your American one. The place came in for attack but was never taken, not even by Cromwell, who used to take whatever fortress he attempted."

"And your family has always been here," put in Gonda.

"Oh, not quite," put in Ensley. "Nothing has always been here. Earth's life has been long and various. But we've lived here from far back in history; one might say well before history. It is always a younger son who lives at Chimney Pots—the Ensleys have a title and a fairly stately home, a good way off to the north." He sipped at his sherry. "I'm the younger son of my generation, you see. My brother, my elder brother, has only one son and is unlikely to have another. So I feel fairly well established here."

"You and all those younger sons before you," said Thunstone. "Does that succession perhaps go back for those ten thousand years?"

"Exactly," said Ensley. "We have certain family traditions, which we take seriously—written records and oral ones. When I was a boy, my elders instructed me in those oral traditions, made me commit many things to memory."

"For ten thousand years?" asked Thunstone again.

"Why not for ten thousand years? Traditions hang on, don't you find? Here, may I give you a little more of this sherry?"

"It's very good, but no thanks."

Thunstone gazed at another of the pictures on the wall. It was an exaggerated representation of a gigantic horned creature, seemingly a bull, in the act of charging at the smaller figure of a man with a poised spear. The bull seemed to be stuck full of spears. The colors were bright brown and black, with strokes of red.

"That's an interesting composition," said Thunstone. "It looks like a painting from a Stone Age cavern."

"It was suggested by just such a painting," said Gonda. She twiddled her glass. Again the jewels sparkled on her hand.

"You've studied prehistoric paintings?" asked Thunstone, interested.

Hob Sayle plodded in, in his white coat. "Dinner is served," he proclaimed.

"Thank you," said Ensley, rising. "Will you come along with me? What we'll have today is fairly simple, even unimaginative. One might say, a representative company dinner in a plain old English home. But I'll warrant it's well cooked. Come on then, follow me."

He escorted Gonda toward the inner door. Thunstone followed. Ensley seated Gonda at the head of the table, with himself and Thunstone to either side.

Mrs. Sayle brought in a tureen, from which she ladled jellied madrilene into bowls for each. Ensley took up a tall bottle and studied the label.

"Ah yes, this is a Portuguese red article. I found some and thought it quite good," he said. "I hope you'll think the same."

Sayle took the bottle and poured a trifle into Ensley's glass. Ensley sniffed it expertly, tasted it, and nodded his head. Sayle went to fill Gonda's glass, then Thunstone's, then returned to finish filling Ensley's.

The madrilene was good and flavory. The three of them finished it and Sayle fetched in a great platter with a splendid-looking rib roast of beef. Ensley took up knife and fork and carved with skill.

"Gonda, my dear, I know you prefer a rare inside slice," he said. "How about you, Mr. Thunstone? Rare, or well done at the end here?"

"I don't have a choice," said Thunstone.

Plates were sent along with generous slices of meat. Mrs. Sayle appeared to offer a dish of squares of hot Yorkshire pudding, another of small roast potatoes, still another of brussels sprouts with butter sauce. Everything was excellent.

"You did wrong to call this a simple dinner, Mr. Ensley," Thunstone said. "It's as fine food as I've had since I came to England."

"When I was a boy, we had a dinner of this sort every Sunday," said Ensley. "How glad I am that you enjoy it. Will either of you have more? No? All right then, Mrs. Sayle, the dessert."

Hob Sayle cleared away the dinner plates, and Mrs. Sayle came in with dishes of strawberries on bits of cake like rich, slightly sweetened American biscuit. The strawberries were crowned with cream so thick as to be clotted, and they were as sweet as sugar. Thunstone praised them, and so did Gonda. Ensley went on with his discussion of the past as they ate.

"I say that my family has traditions that go back too far to be easily believed," he told them. "Things that have been passed down by word of mouth, from long before the invention of writing. From back when Claines existed here, under what name has not survived, and its men took their stone weapons to hunt deer and geese, and more baleful game like bear and wild cattle and wild swine."

He said that in a calm, matter-of-fact tone, as though commenting on something that had happened only the other day.

"Yes," Thunstone agreed, appropriately as he hoped. "Wild cattle and hogs must have been formidable."

"Formidable's the right word," said Ensley. "Strong, fierce animals. They must have taken a considerable taming in later centuries, and at the time we speak of they took a considerable killing. No wonder they were both worshipped as symbols of power—the bull and the boar. And there were other menaces in those ancient thickets —the bears and wolves. But those men had to hunt if they hoped to eat. There was no agriculture here as yet. Ten thousand years ago, it was having its beginnings in the Middle East, but that old aftermath of the last Ice Age still lingered here—short growing seasons, fierce winters. Nobody grew grain or kept herds. They only hunted. And the women gathered what wild fruits and nuts they could find, and edible leaves and seeds."

Plainly Ensley expected to be believed. Thunstone could give himself no good reason to doubt.

"And all this is part of your family tradition," he said to Ensley. "These people you tell of in the Stone Age, they're your ancestors."

"They're the ancestors of all Britain," said Ensley. "Celts came in later, and Romans and Saxons and Danes and Normans, to mingle. But the old blood remains."

"Did any of their language descend?" Thunstone asked. "Naturally they had language. Did some of their words come down to the present?"

"One word at least. A name, to be explicit." Ensley paused as though for effect. "Gram," he said suddenly.

Gonda drew in her breath. "Gram," she repeated. Thunstone waited.

"And so, as you see," went on Ensley, "my given one is an old one. Back in the beginning, it was the name of a god. There has always been someone named Gram in my family." He turned his gaze on Thunstone. "Do you think I'm talking foolishness?" he challenged.

"I hope that I've indicated no such thing," said Thunstone.

"See here," said Ensley, "if we've all had enough dinner, why don't we go back to the sitting room for our coffee? We can talk more comfortably there. And if you remain skeptical, perhaps I can manage to convince you."

They rose with him and walked back to the sitting room together. Hob Sayle followed, balancing a silver tray with a coffee pot, three delicate china cups, a cream jug, and a sugar bowl. He set the tray on a central table.

"Now, Hob, will you bring in that decanter of brandy?" said Ensley. "Sit down, please. Gonda, maybe you'll pour for us."

Gonda filled the cups. "Cream?" she asked Thunstone. "Sugar?"

"Neither, I thank you," he replied, taking his cup. Gonda and Ensley both took cream and sugar. Hob Sayle brought in another tray, with a tall dark bottle and three little silver cups, not greatly larger than thimbles. Ensley unstoppered the bottle and filled the little cups. He lifted his own.

"I'll propose a toast, and I hope you'll join me," he said. "I drink to the nature of reality."

They drank. The brandy, too, was excellent. They returned to their coffee.

"Will you take a good cigar, Mr. Thunstone?" invited Ensley.

"Thank you, I have my pipe," said Thunstone.

Gonda chose a long white cigarette from an enameled box on the coffee table. Thunstone filled his pipe and Ensley lighted a cigar. They finished their coffee as they talked.

"I'll admit, Mr. Thunstone, that some of my claims sound extravagant," said Ensley. "About how old Claines is, and how old my people are in Claines. Gonda here has heard me on the subject, and I think she's more apt to credit me."

"I haven't questioned anything, have I?" Thunstone appealed. "I'm intrigued, naturally, but that's all. I take a great interest in everything you say here."

"We have spoken of visions," reminded Ensley. "Visions of ancient times, back beyond man's memory. Gonda can speak to those if she will."

"Yes," said Gonda, blowing out a pale thread of cigarette smoke. "I have always been able to see into the past. Yes, I paint and play the piano, and I have been on the stage, but I am also a psychic. I have demonstrated that fact to scholars of the occult."

"Which is how I met her, in Stockholm," contributed Ensley. "Which is why I have invited her to Claines, to help in my study of beginnings here. And she has been most helpful. You've admired her paintings, Mr. Thunstone. I wonder, I dare ask myself, if there isn't something in them that you find—shall we say—reminiscent."

He watched Thunstone expectantly. Thunstone looked at the paintings.

"I suppose it's time for me to admit that I've had sensations of what Claines used to be," said Thunstone. "I've never called myself psychic, but I've done considerable research in the field of the supernormal. At night here, when it's fully dark, I've felt the force of antiquities."

"Felt," Ensley echoed him. "Felt. And perhaps seen?"

"Well, yes. That, too."

"You have seen," said Ensley, frankly eager. "I knew it from what you've said and what you've left unsaid."

"Have I been as obvious as all that?" asked Thunstone.

"It may be that I recognize the sensitivity in you," said Ensley. "Because I, too, can see into a far backward reach of man's life on earth."

"I've told you that Constance Bailey can do the same."

"Constance Bailey would have been invited here long ago," Ensley half snorted, "but she's chosen to be my enemy. She claims witch powers, second sight. She's tried to spread rumors about me. She's tried to use spells against me. I've cast her out. Nor do I hold with David Gates's pretenses to scholarship about this community and its history and prehistory. I've heard that he threatened in his sermon today to be downright violent at the turning of the Dream Rock tonight."

"Yes," said Thunstone. "He was quite emphatic."

"Hardly the way for a churchman to act and speak," said Ensley. "And you, sir, you promised to come and help him."

Hob Sayle must have run to Ensley with that news.

"I did say that I'd be there," admitted Thunstone.

Gonda had refilled their brandy cups. "May I offer a toast?" she said. "To no violence."

"Hear, hear," said Ensley, and again they drank together. Ensley got up.

"Mr. Thunstone," he said, "it's high time for me to show you that I don't speak idly about records going back to Stone Age times."

"Ten thousand years ago," said Thunstone once more.

"That long ago, if you wish. Will you and Gonda come with me, then, down into the cellars of Chimney Pots? I promise that you'll find them interesting."

# CHAPTER 14

Ensley raised his voice: "Hob Sayle!" he called.

Sayle came from the dining room. "Sir?"

"Get those electric lanterns," ordered Ensley. "Both of them."

"Yes, sir." Sayle bustled away somewhere and was back with the lanterns. They were impressive lanterns, a foot and a half high, with tubular glass all the way around and bails to carry them by.

"Give me one," said Ensley, reaching his hand for it. "You keep the other. Now then, Gonda, Mr. Thunstone, follow me."

They went into the hall, Sayle bringing up the rear. Ensley led the way to where, at the back, rose a massive door of ancient varnished planks. It had a dull brass lock, in which was a key that looked hand-hammered. Ensley turned the key. The lock rasped powerfully and Ensley drew the door toward him and went into darkness beyond. As he did so he turned on the light he carried.

"Be careful on these steps," he warned. "They're very old—how old they are is one of the things I can't surely tell you about Chimney Pots. But Ensleys were using them before the time of Elizabeth. The first Elizabeth, I mean, the great Elizabeth. Turn on your lantern too, Hob."

Sayle obeyed. Ensley went downward, between masonry walls that clung close on both sides of a narrow descent. Thunstone looked back at Gonda, but she motioned him to go ahead of her, then she followed. Sayle came behind her. The glow of the two electric lanterns danced and crept around them. The steps under Thunstone's soles were narrow and rough, and he was careful in his going down. Gonda's hand rested on his shoulder.

"I've been here before," said her voice in his ear, "but it's a dubious descent."

"Yes," he agreed.

They came out on some sort of landing. The walls were farther apart here. To either side, Thunstone saw shelves cut into rock, and upon them rows of bottles, lying flat, one upon the other.

"Our wine cellar," Ensley informed them. "My people have always been serious about their wine. Even during the war, we were able to keep a good selection here."

"The wine we had at dinner was splendid," said Thunstone.

"But we're on our way to an older selection yet," said Ensley. "Come on, and here we have more stairs. Be rather careful of these, too."

He was right in giving that warning. The steps beyond the wine cellar seemed to be uneven slabs and chunks of rock, roughly plastered into place, and the walls to either side were not of masonry. They seemed to be steep faces of rough stone. Thunstone kept a hand on the one to his right, and Gonda fairly clutched his shoulder. They followed Ensley down, down. Thunstone counted more than thirty steps to another fairly flat surface below.

"Here we are, then," proclaimed Ensley. "More or less."

He lifted his lantern high. Thunstone could see a sort of gallery, rock walls and ceiling that had the look of some ancient wash of water. The walls looked splotched.

"Mr. Thunstone, you and I have touched on the fact that nobody knows of any important cave paintings in Britain," Ensley was saying. "That's because nobody has been allowed to see these except for members of my family. Oh yes, Gonda has been down here, and you've seen an effort she made to do a picture inspired by them. But except for her, you're something of a first here."

He took a couple of steps forward and directed his light on a rise of the wall. "Here," he said, "what do you think of this?"

Thunstone, too, came forward. He looked and Gonda came beside him and looked.

Over the rock was spread a huge picture that at once jogged his memory. It was done in primitive tints, blacks and browns and reds, perhaps worked up from earths of various colors. There the whole scene was, the mighty bull with spears jutting from it, blood pouring from it, charging at the hunter who poised another spear for a cast. A study of that scene was upstairs in Ensley's drawing room.

"Gonda copied this," said Thunstone at once.

"I tried," said Gonda, gazing half-prayerfully. In her black clinging dress, she looked just then like some sort of priestess. "I cannot say if I succeeded."

"What you did was impressive," Thunstone assured her.

"I think I should have tried to use the same paints," Gonda said. "These primitive ones, worked up from earths and charcoals and powdered rocks. Maybe I can try again."

"Maybe, but look here at the next picture," Ensley urged them.

He held his lantern above his head. Its glow revealed another upward surge of the rock, with upon it a stir of various shapes, each shape with its own tinge.

"I do not like the snakes," said Gonda unhappily, and at once Thunstone saw them, twining here and there across the surface. There were half a dozen sprawling bunches of them, their coils and writhings manifest, their heads strongly defined with the deep-set eyes and lumpy jowls that denoted poisonous reptiles. They seemed to be wriggling among plants with leaves and blooms, red, yellow, and blue.

"I've not been able to try an impression of this," Gonda confessed.

"Because of the snakes, but the snakes have their place in the concept," said Ensley. "I've pointed this out before, Gonda. We have here the spring of the year. Because snakes come out in the spring, along with the spring flowers."

"I do not like snakes," she said again. "I am afraid of them."

"Then come along to the next picture. You've seen that too, my dear; you don't turn sick from it."

They had come into a wider corridor in the rock, Thunstone could see by now. Ensley led them around a turn of the way, and again held up his lantern to reveal a painting on the rock.

This was truly colorful. It had a background of sorts, a smearing of green strokes and patches. Against that showed figures in red brown.

An antlered animal with slender legs was manifestly a stag. It was shown in graceful motion, its head was clearly recognizable as a deer's, its antlers were traced to curved points. Behind it followed another deer, smaller and without antlers, plainly a doe. Behind the doe, a fawn balanced on slender legs.

"If that other was meant to be spring, this is summer," said Thunstone.

"Exactly," said Ensley. "The symbolism of nature, do you see? And the work of skillful Stone Age artists. England has such work after all, Mr. Thunstone; the musty scholars just haven't seen it as yet. I've kept it hidden here under my house. Probably you'll call me selfish."

"I won't guess at your motives," Thunstone told him. "But tomorrow, two friends of mine intend to come to Claines. Professor Leslie Spayte of the University of London—"

"Yes, I've seen some things he's written," said Ensley. "A hard laborer in the field of paleontology, though he has much to learn. Tomorrow, you say? But by then, the Dream Rock will have been turned. And who's your other friend?"

"His name is Philo Vickery."

"I don't know it."

"Philo is a novelist. He writes about antiquarian and folklore subjects. He'd like to develop into a sort of latter-day Thomas Hardy. And he'd love to see these treasures."

"Tomorrow may be too late for him to come," said Ensley cryptically. "Look along the bottom border of this summer scene, Mr. Thunstone, and tell me what you see."

Thunstone looked. "A long row of what looks like small hands, done in black pigment," he said.

"Five-fingered hands, is that right? Count them."

Stooping, Thunstone did so. "Eighteen hands," he said after a moment. "And a single stroke at the end of the line."

"And eighteen times five is—" prompted Ensley.

"Ninety," said Gonda. "Gram you showed me these pictures, but never that line of hands."

"Ninety plus one is more or less the number of days in a summer," said Ensley. "Had I called your attention to it, you'd have seen a similar row of five-fingered hands at the bottom of the one for spring. Those old people, you begin to understand, had a good sense of the progression of the seasons. Now look across here, at the wall opposite."

He swung his lantern that way. Another picture leaped into view.

This was brightly colored, great splashes of ocher and two shades of red, with here and there touches of russet brown. There seemed to be an effort to depict autumn leaves in rich, contrasting tints. Upright black streaks indicated the trunks of the trees that bore these glories, and below them were more huddles and swirls of color, as though to represent fallen leaves. But the focus of the scene was a pair of stags, vigorously locking antlers in a lively representation of a fight.

"Then this is autumn," said Thunstone at once. "The season of what American Indians called the Mad Moon. When stags fight, sometimes to the death."

"That action is marvelous," said Gonda raptly. "In fall, the *hreinn* —the reindeer will fight, yes and sometimes kill each other, in Norway. Even those we think are tame."

"And another string of hand-figures to count the days," said Thunstone, pointing. "Winter, I suppose, is the next mural."

"It is indeed the next," said Ensley. "Right here, just beyond autumn."

The scene his lantern showed them was rather narrow from side to side, and most of it was so pallid as to seem blank. But that, Thunstone saw quickly, was to represent snow, and a lot of it. If the artist had worked ten thousand years ago, winters were bitter then, frequently with blizzards. Central in the composition stood a snow-burdened tree, plainly an evergreen, for there were blotches of spinach-colored foliage visible through the clots of snow upon the branches.

At the foot of the tree half-sprawled, half-crouched something massive and dark. It was recognizable as a bear, and from it jutted a long black line that would have to be the haft of a spear that transfixed it. Off to the side, not so immediately noticeable as the tree and the bear, stood two rather sketchy human figures. One of them held another spear, raised and ready to throw. They were hunters, in at their kill.

"I feel sorry for the poor bear," said Gonda.

So did Thunstone, whose many adventures had never included the hunting and killing of a bear. He had in his time known bear hunters who had assured him that bear meat was delicious, tender, could even be smoked into savory ham or bacon. In any case, killing bears in the Stone Age winter would be desirable, necessary. Then, as in this century, hunger was the silent enemy in the cold months.

"And that's what winter was like," said Thunstone, gazing at the picture. "Down here in the snowy foreground, again we have our row of little hands—enough, I imagine, to make ninety fingers in all. Yes, and a couple of points more than that."

"You see things well, Mr. Thunstone," said Ensley. "These four seasonal impressions denote the progress of a year, and to count all the points gives us the number of days in a year. Stone Age people were able to compute such matters, do you agree, then? Some thousands of years after these pictures, others built Stonehenge, which accurately indicates the progress of the year, which notices the phases of the moon, which foretells eclipses. Our ancestors were not savages. They were, in their way, scientists."

"And you've never allowed anyone to see these wonders," said Thunstone.

"I've brought Gonda down here to look, to copy. And now I've brought you."

"I hope you'll let me bring my friends Spayte and Vickery when they come tomorrow."

"Tomorrow," echoed Ensley, almost dreamily. "Who knows what tomorrow will be like? But today, there is more to show you in this cavern."

"More?" said Gonda, standing back beside Hob Sayle.

"I've never taken you past this point, my dear, but we'll go have a look now, all of us."

He moved along, lantern in hand. He stopped again. "Look," he said. "Look at what's here."

Hob Sayle had brought his own lantern close. The two lights

revealed a long, high stretch of pale gray rock, patterned all over in a strange fashion.

"What is it?" Thunstone asked.

"What would you guess?" asked Ensley in turn.

Thunstone put his hand to the rock. "Here's a sort of tally," he said. "Here we have a row of marks, one above the other, cut into the rock."

He moved his big forefinger along.

"Ten of them here, like the ten painted marks in that Welsh cave we were talking about. And an upright line running through them, and right next another arrangement of ten, and more beyond that, and below and above. Groups of ten and ten and ten." He looked at Ensley. "A tally of some sort. A record."

Ensley smiled and nodded. "As you say, a tally, a record. Of what, would you guess?"

"All I can do is guess, but it's a big record." Thunstone looked at the long, high spread of markings. He put his hand up to the topmost groupings. It was as high as a tall man could reach, and perhaps twenty feet long, perhaps more.

"There are thousands of markings, all in tens," he said.

"And if you look, you'll see the tens grouped in hundreds," said Ensley. "And the hundreds in thousands."

"Could there be ten thousand of them?" asked Thunstone. "Is this a record of your ten thousand years?"

"Not quite," said Ensley. "To be exact, nine thousand, nine hundred and ninety-nine, if you care to count. A single tally mark more here," and, stooping, he touched one string of notches at the bottom of the far end of the display, "will make it exactly ten thousand." He straightened and faced them. "Ten thousand years, Gonda. Ten thousand years, Mr. Thunstone. The last thirty years or so, I myself have notched into the record, with a modern hammer and chisel."

He pointed his finger. At the base of the great arrangement of notches lay a short-handled hammer and a cold chisel, dull gray in his lantern light.

"Ready to supply the last notch, ready to make up the even ten thousand," said Ensley. "Again, do you care to count and make sure?"

"I'll take your word for it," said Thunstone, and Gonda nodded agreement in the halo of light cast by Hob Sayle's lantern. "But maybe you'll explain now the full significance of these ten thousand years."

"Those marks record the length of a sleep, a very, very long sleep. The sleep of Gram."

"Gram?" Gonda cried. "But you are Gram."

"Only a namesake," said Ensley, with an air of patient explanation. "Didn't I speak of the god Gram at dinner? To be sure I did. Very well. Gram lives but he sleeps. These marks record the passage of the years of his slumber. Do you see now?"

Thunstone stood silent. Ensley faced toward him.

"I persist in feeling that you find my statements hard to believe, Mr. Thunstone."

He waited. Thunstone did not speak.

"I see," said Ensley gently. "I see. You're too polite to say that you find all this extravagant. Perhaps, if I showed you where Gram sleeps away his hundred centuries?"

"I'd be interested in seeing such a place," said Thunstone.

"We're on our way there. The passage makes another bend, here ahead. Just follow me along."

As before, he led the way and Sayle brought up the rear. Beyond the turn, just past that sea of markings, the rocks on either side were closer in, making the way narrow.

"Bring your lantern up front, Hob," ordered Ensley. "Now, what do we find?"

The way ahead narrowed again, sharply. It seemed to be closed by an arrangement of broad squares, the size of books. The borders of the squares were heavy bars of rusted iron. It was like a cell front in a prison.

"Gram sleeps there," said Ensley. "Come close. Don't be afraid; he won't stir for any noise you make just now."

They were all at the grid of bars. "Hold up your lantern, Hob, and keep it high," directed Ensley.

He set his own lantern down on the rocky floor and fumbled at something on the grid. A harsh grating resounded, as of a lock opening. Ensley caught the barred door and dragged it toward him and against the side of the cavern.

"Now," he said, "look in and see what you see."

It was a rough-walled cavern, more or less the size of the room Mrs. Fothergill used for office and parlor. At the rear, hard to see in the gloom of the place, rose what looked like a great dark boulder as big as a small car, shaped like a huge loaf of burnt bread.

"There are candles inside," Ensley was saying. "One on that little shelf next the big case there, where Gram is at rest. Go and light it for us, Gonda."

He took her by the elbow and urged her forward. She took several hesitant steps past the door.

"I can see the candle," she said, "but I haven't a match."

"Here," said Thunstone, following her in and holding out his matchbox.

Behind him rose a whine of rusty hinges. Next moment, the scrape of the lock again.

# CHAPTER 15

Thunstone whirled around and lunged at the bars. They creaked and sang at the impact of his big body, but they did not yield. They had been locked in place. On the far side of them, Ensley had drawn a couple of paces away. His bright electric lantern gleamed in his left hand. In his right he held a key nearly the size of a hairbrush.

"You can't get out," he said. "Neither you nor Gonda. Those bars were put up in Queen Victoria's time, but they will hold."

"Unlock this damned door!" shouted Thunstone.

"No, that would spoil everything. There are excellent reasons for you two to stay where you are."

"Well, I'm not staying here." Thunstone seized the thick bars in his hand and shook the door so that it grated on its hinges. "There's such a thing as law in this country, and you're breaking it by locking us up."

"What the law will be in this country, after midnight tonight, is an interesting conjecture," said Ensley mildly. "Shall I explain?"

"Do," said Thunstone, and again strained at the bars.

Behind him he heard Gonda make a noise, a sort of strangled swallow. Out in the corridor, Hob Sayle held his lantern well to the rear of Ensley.

"Suppose we go back to how things were here, those ten thousand years ago," began Ensley. "Almost exactly ten thousand years ago, within short hours. There were only these caves here then, and they were the temple of Gram."

"He was worshipped," said Thunstone.

"Yes, he was worshipped indeed. The hunting community that lived here—in fairly snug huts and roofed-over hollows scattered over this part of what has become Claines—worshipped him. He was helpful to his worshippers. Showed where good game was—deer, cattle, wild geese. Showed where to spear fish in pools and streams. When other tribes made war, Gram helped his worshippers win. Yes, he was worshipped. Those old, old paintings you have seen were painted to his honor and glory. And he accepted sacrifices made in gratitude." Ensley paused, as though to time his next words to sink in. "Human sacrifices," he said then.

"What kind of human sacrifices?" asked Thunstone. "Prisoners of war?"

"Oh, no. Prisoners were never taken in war in those days. The sacrifices were people of the tribe, special people. People who could dream dreams, see visions." Again a pause. "People like you, Mr. Thunstone, and Gonda, too."

Again Gonda made a wretched sound in her throat. She seemed to try to speak, and to fail at it.

"Was Gram visible?" Thunstone asked, close against the bars. "What was he like, if people saw him? Like you, the Gram of today?"

"Nothing so matter-of-fact as that. He was a god, you see. He was very tall and broad, twice the size of a mortal man. Shaggy with hair, like a beast, but not a beast. On his head—horns, the branched horns of a stag. An impressive figure."

"You talk as though you've seen him."

"I have. I can look backward through time. Ten thousand years ago, I'd have been a logical sacrifice to Gram."

"You're descended from him," said Thunstone, as though making a charge.

"If that's true, I can hardly assemble a genealogy when there are no written records anywhere." Ensley seemed almost to be chatting, as though they were sitting together upstairs with glasses of brandy. "But back then, ten thousand years ago—"

"You've assured yourself that I've been there," broke in Thunstone.

"Simply by observing you, listening to you, putting quite a column of twos and twos together. Gonda has been back in that time, too. And I with her."

"I didn't notice you there."

"But I noticed you. I saw you kill two men, two highly respected community members. That act should logically forfeit your own life, Mr. Thunstone. Well, then, all three of us have the gift of seeing back in time, adventuring back in time. That's why I speak to the point now."

Gonda had come to Thunstone's side. She, too, held the bars with her slim hands. "Gram," she said, "you can't leave us penned up here."

"I fear that I must," he replied gently. "This is the end of that ten thousand years we keep talking about. At midnight, the end."

"You're crazy," Thunstone said.

"Don't use that word to me," Ensley snapped. "You wanted me to tell you. Be still and I'll do so."

Thunstone said no more, nor did Gonda. Ensley cleared his throat and began to speak again.

"Gram looked after his own. In those Stone Age days, he provided that the hunters found meat, that the women could gather fruits and berries and nuts and seeds; saw that there was wood for fires in the cold seasons. That no conquering enemy should conquer here. And then, Gram grew weary. He said that he would sleep for ten thousand years."

"There you go again," said Thunstone, wishing that his arm was long enough for a grab at the lapel of Ensley's beautifully cut coat. "Ten thousand years again."

"Once more in all patience I ask, let me explain," said Ensley. "Gram had prospered his people, had savored the grateful sacrifices they had made, until a certain time was accomplished. What the time was, or why it had to end, I can't fully explain, but Gram lay down to sleep. He said he would sleep for ten thousand years. A count must be kept, and you have seen that it has been kept. Each year, the stone image made of him by the priests of the tribe must be turned over, so that he could rest easily."

"The Dream Rock," said Thunstone.

"Yes. And at the end of the ten thousand years he would wake up to new deeds. New powers. The world would be his world again."

"Which means now."

"Yes, now. Tomorrow, in the first moments of morning after midnight, when the Dream Rock is turned."

"And you believe all this?" said Thunstone.

"I believe. Don't you?"

"What will the world change into?"

"Wouldn't some sort of change be good?" Ensley flung back.

"Change back to ten thousand years ago?" Thunstone challenged.

"Might that not be a good change?" said Ensley. "Something other than this modern civilized world, this desperate, insane world, that teeters on the edge of destroying itself? The world of Gram and his people again, that survived and improved and prevailed."

Thunstone made no reply to that. Ensley chuckled, then went on:

"When the Dream Rock is turned over there," he said, "Gram will waken and rise from where he sleeps. Rise and find you two here, you and Gonda."

"What have I done to you?" Gonda whimpered. "Why do you trick me in here and shut me up?"

"I've explained that, Gonda," said Ensley, with an air of gentle patience. "Gram will want you both when he wakens. Thunstone for food, logically. You—maybe for love."

She began to cry.

"Ensley," said Thunstone, "you'll wind up paying with your life for this."

"Many will wind up paying for this with their lives," said Ensley. "The world has changed so greatly since Gram went to sleep. Think how it will change when he rises up."

"How?" growled Thunstone.

"Wait and see."

Thunstone's hand quested to the lock. It was of massive iron, set solidly into the barred door, with a keyhole big enough to admit his forefinger. Thunstone dragged at the lock. It did not even budge in its place.

"You're a very strong man, but you'll never force that," said Ensley. "Hob and I saw to it and the hinges too, not long ago. You can't get out without this." He held up the key triumphantly. "You'll be there when Gram wakes."

He began to back away along the corridor, with Hob Sayle.

"I'll get out, all right," promised Thunstone grimly.

"Hob will be on guard hereabouts at all times," returned Ensley. "Later in the evening, he'll bring you something to eat and drink. But don't try to grapple him through the bars. He won't have the key, won't be able to open the door."

The two backed away farther.

"You have hours as yet," Ensley called. "Why not tell each other the stories of your lives?"

The lantern looked dim by then.

"Quick, let's light the candle," said Thunstone to Gonda. "Where did I drop those matches?"

Stooping, he groped along the rocky floor and found the box. He struck a match and held it to the wick of a candle as thick as his wrist, stuck in its own wax to a projection of the wall. The flame rose, clear and lean and lemon yellow, like the petal of a flower. It gave them a soft radiance.

Gonda had sat down on a lower shelf of rock against the wall. She seemed to crouch there, to cower. She lifted her face. It looked ghostly.

"And now what?" she asked in a dead voice. "How are we to get out of here?"

"We'll see," said Thunstone. "Someone or other said that if you get into a place, you can get out. We'll see."

He turned this way and that, making a study of their prison in the gentle light.

At the rear of it, opposite the barred door, was a hollowed niche and within that the dark boulder. That stone seemed to be a dozen feet long and six feet high, and it almost filled the recess. Coming closer to see his best, Thunstone saw that on top of it lay a separate slab of rock, like a lid. He put both hands to that, and heaved. It seemed to stir. He took his hands away and put his ear to the lower mass.

He could hear something. Something slow and regular, like deep breathing. He faced around toward Gonda.

"I don't think we'd better lift that upper rock just now," he said. "Ensley spoke this much truth. Something's asleep inside."

"Horrible," moaned Gonda. "Horrible, horrible."

She still cowered where she sat. Thunstone made note of other things. Chief among these, more candles stuck here and there, in cracks or niches of the rock.

"We'll be glad we have these," he said, gathering them up.

"Once Ensley brought me almost here," said Gonda. "He wanted to do a sort of worship by those lights. Four, five, he lighted them. The way he acted frightened me. I ran back upstairs, and later he came up and laughed and said I didn't understand."

"I'm beginning to understand," said Thunstone. "I'm convinced. I wouldn't be if I hadn't seen back across his ten thousand years."

He went again to the barred doorway. Carefully he studied it, in the beam of his pocket flashlight. It was strongly hinged into the rock, with bolts sunk deeply into the stone of the wall. The lock, as he had seen, as Ensley had said, was of iron too sturdy for him to budge. He turned away from the examination of the door to face Gonda.

"We'll have to see what happens," he said. "May I smoke my pipe?"

"Please," she said. "Please do. I'll have a cigarette; I brought some."

He filled the pipe and held the end of the burnt match to the candle flame to light her cigarette, then the pipe. Her face was a taut, pallid mask in the glow of the match. She sat down on a fragment of rock close to the wall. Thunstone leaned near the niche where the boulder and its lid lay. Both of them smoked in silence. Then:

"Tell each other the stories of our lives, he said," remembered Gonda. "I'm not afraid to tell mine."

"And I'm not afraid to listen, and tell mine in turn," said Thunstone.

"It always begins, a life story, by telling where the teller was born, and when. My birthplace was a small town on the coast of Norway,

Fredrikshal, but then we moved to Oslo, where my mother brought me up to win contests."

Her mother, it seemed, early recognized that Gonda had several talents. Gonda was given piano lessons, and competed for prizes. Gonda was taught to paint, and entered her canvases in various exhibitions. And Gonda had power to read the pasts and futures of visitors and neighbors, and became a spiritistic medium and earned money at that, money which her mother was glad to appropriate.

She did not mention a father, though she must have had one. Thunstone wondered, but did not ask, if she might be illegitimate. She went on to say that she grew to womanhood and refused to let her mother keep the money that she, Gonda, earned. She traveled to Paris, to Vienna, to exhibit her mediumistic gifts. She attracted some attention, at theaters and at homes of rich enthusiasts. Men admired her. She hinted that she had had lovers, though she did not name them, did not go into detail. At last, a year or so ago, she had met Gram Ensley.

"And he was charming," she said. "You have seen that he can be plausible, persuasive. He told me of a field of psychical research to study here. He offered me money to come. No, he never made love to me. But almost at once, he found that I could see back into the long-ago times. He found that we could go there together."

"Then you've both traveled back ten thousand years."

"We have. I can do it by turning out all lights. If we blew out that candle—it's almost out now—"

Thunstone went to the candle. It was burned almost to its end; her story had taken more time than he thought. He rummaged, found another stump and lighted its wick from the first, and stuck it to the rock. Returning to Gonda, he studied her pale face, her pale hair. "Tell the rest," he urged her.

"Not much to tell. He brought me down to look at those paintings you saw. He was happy when I tried some studies from them. And he has liked my playing on his piano. He promised to introduce me to someone of great fascination." Her slant eyes studied him. "Did he mean you, did he foresee you would come to Claines?"

"Or did he mean Gram, lying there, due to waken?" suggested Thunstone.

She shuddered. Even in the dim blur of light, she looked fine-figured in her black dress. The coal of a fresh cigarette glowed to reflect from her eyes.

"Your turn now," she said. "Your story. Turnabout is fair play."

Thunstone sat down on the rough floor, his back against a rise of the rock. He felt a chill in the air, as though from some deep chasm somewhere. Might that chasm be found, might it spell freedom? He looked at Gonda in the flicker of the candle's beam, and told what he felt like telling of his life story.

It was a story that started in fairly simple terms. His had been a modest country upbringing, an early growth to size and strength that found him working between school terms at a lumberyard, a slaughterhouse, a sawmill; a chance to go to college because his tuition would be paid, his expenses most modestly met, if he would play football; graduate work after that, then his fortunate meeting with Judge Keith Hilary Pursuivant, their friendship and partnership in strange activities; his adventures against creatures that called themselves the Shonokins, that claimed to have owned America before the first Indian comers, whose claims at times seemed valid, whose efforts took a considerable lot of defeating. He told Gonda that he liked small comforts in life, good food and drink, pleasant, sensible talk with pleasant, sensible people, and that he hoped eventually for peace and quiet.

As he finished, the second candle guttered almost into darkness. Quickly Thunstone searched here and there, found yet another big stump, and lighted it. He looked at his watch in its radiance.

"Seven o'clock, or nearly," he said. "Over yonder I see one more piece of candle. Maybe we'll have candlelight enough to see until midnight."

"Why are there candles here?" asked Gonda.

"You've answered that. Ensley conducted religious rites, here around this tomb, or couch, call it what you like."

He went close to the great mass of rock. He leaned his ear against it and heard a blurred rush of sound, a pause, another rush. It was as though something inside breathed rhythmically.

"What do you hear?" Gonda whispered.

"Nothing much," he lied, coming away from the boulder.

She clenched her fists. "Oh," she said tautly, "I could scream, scream at the top of my lungs."

"I hope you don't," said Thunstone. "You might wake up whatever's nesting yonder, wake it up before midnight."

She relaxed a trifle, but only a trifle. She rose to her feet.

"One thing I did not hear in your life story," she said. "Mention of women."

"I've known various women," he told her, "but I didn't feel like dragging them into my story."

She looked at him, slant-eyed, pallid-faced. Her mouth was held so tightly he could barely see her lips.

"Did you hear Gram Ensley when he left us here?" she said. "He spoke of death, he spoke of love. He himself never made love to me— but I've said that, haven't I? I wonder, did he mean that you and I should make love?"

She came closer at that. She breathed deeply. She fixed her eyes on him.

"If he meant that," said Thunstone, "I'd certainly never make love at Ensley's command."

"Do you know what love is?" she half-cried at him. "Have you ever been in love?"

"I'm in love at this moment," said Thunstone. "I've gone away from her in America because I don't want to involve her in the things I do—things like what I'm doing here. If I can be glad of anything here and now, I'm glad she's not in this place with us, waiting for whatever will happen."

Gonda looked out through the bars. "Somebody's coming," she said.

A light bobbed in the tunnel-like hall of rock. Thunstone moved close to the bars. A figure came toward him. It was Hob Sayle, with his electric lantern slung on an elbow. In both hands he bore a heaped tray.

"Mr. Ensley told me to fetch you supper," he said. "I'm coming close, to give things in, but it's no use your trying to lay hold on me. Even if I wanted to unlock for you, I haven't the key."

He slid a bottle between the bars to Thunstone. "That's hock," he said. "I've taken the cork out, so that it can breathe."

"Hold this," said Thunstone to Gonda, putting the bottle in her hands.

"And here, beef sandwiches," said Sayle, handing in napkin-wrapped rectangles. "Cut from the joint we had at dinner."

"Do me a favor," said Thunstone, and passed a sandwich back. "Eat this."

Hob Sayle squinted in the lantern light, and smiled wispily. "Oh, to be sure," he said. "I see what you mean—drugs or poison. It will be a pleasure, sir."

He unwrapped the sandwich and took a big bite.

"Tell me," said Thunstone, "how do you hope to get away with this? Keeping us prisoner here?"

"I do what Mr. Ensley bids me," said Sayle, eating. "I've done that since I was just a lad here. I'm a good soldier."

"You believe in him, and in Gram?" asked Thunstone.

"I do, sir."

He finished the sandwich.

"And now," said Thunstone, taking the bottle back from Gonda, "drink some of this."

"A pleasure, sir," said Sayle again. He turned up the bottle and Thunstone heard it gurgle. "First-rate," said Sayle, giving the bottle back.

"Thanks, and I had to try you," said Thunstone. "Now we'll eat and drink without suspicion."

"You've five hours to midnight, or nearly."

Sayle plodded away, taking his light with him.

Thunstone and Gonda ate their sandwiches and drank from the bottle by turns. They talked. Gonda spoke of love, Thunstone spoke of escape.

"If we're to escape, why don't you find out how?" Gonda prodded him.

"I've looked at everything. The fastenings of the gate, the rocks of the walls. I've looked everywhere but in that hollow rock back in the niche."

He moved toward it.

"Don't open it up," Gonda quavered.

"No. It's supposed to open by itself at midnight."

"When they turn the Dream Rock over," said Gonda tonelessly. "And Gram, the god Gram, wakens up here."

They took turns at the bottle, a sip at a time. When they had finished it, the burning candle was burned down to a fraction of an inch. Thunstone found the last stub. He lighted it with one of his matches, and with the same match kindled a cigarette for Gonda, then his pipe. He did not comment on the old nervousness attending three lights from a match. He bent to study his watch.

"It's just past nine o'clock," he reported.

"Which gives us less than three hours," she scolded. "Why don't you do something? What are you staring at?"

"Somebody's coming," he replied. "Not Hob Sayle this time. At least, it's not his light."

The glow in the corridor slid here and there. "Hello?" called a voice that Thunstone knew.

"Constance Bailey!" he shouted back.

She came at a scuttling run, dressed in her rumpled brown, flourishing a huge electric flashlight the size of a policeman's truncheon.

# CHAPTER 16

Breathlessly, Constance Bailey threw herself against the heavy grid of bars.

"I had to find you," she gasped out. "Mrs. Fothergill was worried—proper prone, she was—you hadn't come to supper, you must be in some kind of trouble."

"I was," said Thunstone.

"And she carried on so, when it got to be nine, I said I'd go look, and I came here. Nobody at the door, but when I came in that Hob Sayle man came in my way and said, 'No, you can't go down there,' and I just hit him a good hard knock with this." She held up the big flashlight. "I'd brought it because the dark was coming, and—"

"You knocked him cold?" put in Thunstone. "Good girl, brave girl."

"We can't get out," Gonda was babbling. "No key—"

"Constance," said Thunstone. "I left my walking cane in the hall upstairs. I leant it against the suit of armor. Go bring it down. If Hob Sayle is trying to come to, hit him another lick."

She was away on twinkling, racing feet. Gonda gave a low moan, as though despairing of any help. Thunstone waited. Back bustled Constance Bailey with the cane. She pushed it between the bars.

"Old Hob hadn't even stirred in his sleep," she reported.

"Thanks," said Thunstone, and drew the blade from the shank. "Hold your light close so that I can see the lock."

She did so. He inserted the silver point, quested inside the lock with it. He felt it grate, felt something yield. The lock moaned, something like Gonda. The door swung open. At once Thunstone pushed it wide.

"How did you do that?" Gonda asked him.

"This blade is holy; it's freed me from danger before," he said. "Now, out with you. I'll be along in a moment."

Gonda's black-clad figure slid out of the enclosed cave like a fleeting shadow. Thunstone, silver blade in hand, walked back to Gram's tomb like resting place.

He pushed at the lid like slab. It was heavy, so heavy that he had to lean his blade against the rock and lift with all the strength of both hands. The slab seemed to grate, to complain as though long centuries had made it adhere to its place. Thunstone exerted all the power of his arms and shoulder muscles, heaved it up to stand on its side like an open lid to a trunk.

Darkness inside, like a pool of ink, and a smell like ancient decay. He looked in, but could see nothing. From his breast pocket he took the small flashlight and directed its beam into the space.

It seemed nearly full of hair, that space. The hair stirred, stirred again, it was dark hair, coarse hair. Whatever the ancient hollow contained, it breathed. Thunstone bent above it, directed his beam here and there. He saw horns. They were pale, branched horns, the color of old ivory. They quivered, just a trifle. They showed where some sort of head must be.

Thunstone took up his blade again and poised its point above the shaggy mass. He could only make a sort of guess as to where to drive it. Down he thrust, powerfully. He felt the point pierce a softness. He put his other palm to the crooked handle and resolutely pushed down, down.

A whining sigh rose, as of escaping air. Thunstone almost choked with the odor that rose around him. He saw the shaggy bulk of the thing fall, collapse, as though it had been deflated. He cleared his blade—it came away easily—and he stepped away. Reaching up with his left hand, he caught the edge of the lid like slab and dragged at it. The thing fell back into place with a loud clap.

Quickly he, too, walked out through the open door. He fished out a handkerchief and wiped his silver blade and dropped the handkerchief. Then he set the blade back into its sheathing shank. Out in the corridor waited Constance Bailey and Gonda. Both of them trembled in the gleam of the flashlight.

"Wh-what was that?" stammered Gonda.

"That was Gram," Thunstone said. "I tried to finish him, but I can't be sure. Maybe the finish must come outside. Show us to the stairs, Constance."

She scurried ahead. Gonda seemed unsteady on her feet and Thunstone took her elbow to help her. She leaned against him.

"Safe?" she whispered. "Are we safe now?"

"I doubt if anyone's safe as yet. Here, these are the stairs."

Up they went, close behind Constance Bailey. The door was open at the top, and they found themselves in the hall. Hob Sayle was there, sitting limply in a corner. He held both hands to his head. Thunstone stopped and leaned above him.

"How do you feel?" he asked.

"Not good," mumbled Sayle. "Not good at all. How did you get out, sir? You must go back there."

"Nothing of the sort," said Thunstone.

"You must," insisted Sayle, rocking his body as he sat. "I'll be done for if you don't."

"I'll be done for if I do," Thunstone snapped. "Sorry, but I have to think of myself. Good night, Sayle."

He went to where Gonda and Constance Bailey stood by the suit of armor. He caught up the heavy mallet that leaned there.

"This might come in handy," he said. "Here, Constance, would you like my cane to carry? You've seen the silver blade in it, you've seen it do wonders."

"It's magic," said Constance Bailey, taking the cane. "Good magic —white magic."

"And now I'll head for the church and the Dream Rock," said Thunstone. "You ladies don't need to come if you don't want to."

"I'm coming," said Constance Bailey.

"I wouldn't dare stay by myself," whimpered Gonda.

"All right."

Thunstone dragged open the front door. Outside, the air was dusky with twilight. Here and there a window glowed, streetlights winked. Constance Bailey went out with Thunstone, her flashlight in hand.

"That's right, keep your beam on," said Thunstone. "Neither you nor I want to slip back out of the twentieth century just now."

The three of them crossed the lawn and then Trail Street and turned toward St. Jude's. They heard a hubbub of voices; they saw a dark blotch of people close together.

Quickening his pace, Thunstone moved ahead of the two women and toward the outskirts of the weaving, chattering crowd. He estimated as many as ninety people there, a larger gathering than had gone to church, indeed a considerable part of the population of Claines. He almost ran into Ensley, who stood a trifle apart from the main press.

"Hello," said Thunstone, and Ensley turned and stared.

"You got out somehow," he said, "but you're too late now. We'll turn the rock, and Gram will rise and rule."

"I wonder," said Thunstone. "Go back to your caves under your house and see if he will rise."

"He will rise," promised Ensley.

Thunstone shoved on toward the center of things, the heavy mallet in his hands. Roughly dressed men crowded close around the Dream Rock, but Gates stood strongly astride the prone pillar. His coat was off, he was in clerical collar and vest. He had turned up the sleeves of his white shirt. He was the biggest man of the assembly, except for Porrask. Porrask towered among companions. In his hand he carried an ax. The beams of the rising moon touched the ax's brown rustiness.

"I forbid you to touch it," Gates was fairly thundering. "I'll keep you from touching it!"

"Ruddy great chance of that, I don't think!" Porrask yelled back at him. "It'll be done, whether you forbid or not!"

Gates swung his head to glare at Porrask. "You want to try it? I'll fight you—you tried to fight a couple of nights ago; you got beaten."

"Not time yet to turn it," called Ensley from back in the crowd. "A couple of hours yet till midnight. Then—"

His voice was drowned in a ragged chorus of cheers. Thunstone shoved a man out of his way and came to where Gates stood.

"I told you I'd help you," he said to Gates.

"Thanks," said Gates between his teeth. Then, again to Porrask: "Want to fight, do you, my man? Fighting's something I was good at in my time. Or would you rather try it on with Thunstone again, and wind up as you did before?"

"Face up to him, Al," called someone in the crowd.

"Time ain't yet," said Porrask, clutching the ax. "But I say to all witnesses, if I'm attacked I'll use that, and it'll be self-defense, that's the word."

"Exactly," said the voice of Ensley. "You're entitled to defend yourself, Porrask. But after tonight, you won't need me to stand with you."

Gates and Porrask faced each other balefully. Porrask's beard bristled; his eyes were wide and fierce.

"Put that thing down," commanded Gates.

"Make me," threw back Porrask, and lifted the ax.

Gates sprang over the Dream Rock and at Porrask. Both his own hands clutched the helve of the ax. Porrask cursed chokingly as the two of them whirled and strove at each other. They slammed into a man in the crowd, bounced off. Then Porrask cursed again as Gates sprang clear of him, the ax in his hands.

Yells went up all around. Gates yelled loudly enough to dominate the others.

"Now!" he roared. "I've taken your ax away, Porrask!"

"And you'll use it on him?" challenged Ensley, coming close among the others. "Strike him with an ax, and call yourself a man of God!"

"I won't use it on him!"

Gates whirled the ax aloft and brought it down on the Dream Rock, with a sound like splitting wood. The blade drove deeply into a vein of the image, sank almost to its eye. That had been a powerful blow. Silence all around for a moment, while Gates dragged on the ax to free it, and could not.

Again people talked, jeered, all through the gathering:

"Ow, old Dream Rock's got your ruddy ax now!"

"Can't fetch it away, can you?"

Again Gates strove to wrench the ax free. It hung in its lodgment as though rooted there.

"Now then," blustered Porrask. "You truly want to try it with me, just fists?"

"Gladly," said Gates, and let go of the ax helve. He straightened up and fixed his eyes on Porrask, as though looking for a place to plant a blow.

Everybody watched them, everybody but Thunstone. He stepped close to the Dream Rock. He planted his feet, tightened his hands on the haft of the mallet, whipped it high above him, and with all his strength he slammed it down on the flat back of the ax's head.

The sound of the impact crashed out like a great clap of thunder, and something like a gale of wind hurled Thunstone back from where he stood. He staggered half a dozen paces, barely keeping his feet. And he was aware of a swift, brief surge of light, as though fire had sprung up for a moment in the dusk, there where the Dream Rock was—

Where the Dream Rock had been. It had shivered into fragments.

That same instant, a woman's voice cried out shrilly.

"Look at Mr. Ensley! Oh, help!"

The crowd stirred. Everyone pulled away from where Ensley had fallen, where he lay limp and motionless and somehow smaller than he had been a moment ago, in life.

"He's struck dead!" screamed someone. "And up there—look!"

On Sweepside, where the gathering gloom should have cloaked Old Thunder, flames danced upward. Thunstone stared at them. They had blue in their red. Once he had seen flames like that, where a gas well had caught fire. Old Thunder burned, as the Dream Rock had burned just a moment ago, before the light there had winked out.

"Judgment of heaven!" Gates called loudly. "Judgment of heaven upon false gods!"

Thunstone dropped his mallet. He went to where Ensley lay, with all others drawn back from him. Kneeling, he drew back an eyelid with his thumb.

"Yes," said Thunstone, rising and wiping his thumb on the skirt of his jacket. "He's dead."

"Dead!" screamed a woman, staring. It was Mrs. Sayle. She swung close to Thunstone. "You killed him!"

"Yes—" gobbled Porrask, making a move toward Thunstone.

"Don't anybody touch him!" warned Constance Bailey, at Thunstone's side. She held the silver blade from the cane, threatened with its keen point.

"Now then, what's all this?" demanded the authoritative voice of Dymock, as he strode into the center of things. "Easy does it, Connie. What's going on here?"

A dozen voices clamored, trying to tell him.

"Mr. Ensley fell dead," Thunstone almost shouted to make Dymock hear. "He was up to something—"

"Something uncanny," chimed in Gates. "When the Dream Rock shattered, why, down he fell."

People quieted again. Dymock stooped above Ensley's motionless body. His hands quested expertly. He straightened again.

"Shattered," he reported. "His bones are shattered, all through. Somebody bring something to cover him. He must lie there until we get help from Gerrinsford."

"I'll bring a spread from my study," volunteered Gates.

"And will you telephone police headquarters at Gerrinsford?" asked Dymock. "Tell them to bring along a doctor to make an examination. I must stay here."

"I'll stay with you," said Constance Bailey.

She held out Thunstone's cane, the blade sheathed again, and he took it. He saw Dymock put his arm around Constance Bailey, as though it belonged there.

"Where can I go?" Gonda babbled to Thunstone. "Not back to Chimney Pots, never."

"We'll both wait here for an inspector or somebody from Gerrinsford," Thunstone said. "They'll have questions to ask us. After that, I'd hope that Mrs. Fothergill can give you a bed tonight."

And it was noon on Monday, bright, English July. Thunstone sat with Spayte and Vickery in the Moonraven, eating sliced ham and drinking beer. Thunstone's friends had checked in at Mrs. Fothergill's, where Gonda had gone to bed the night before and had not come out of her room since.

"Capital ham, this," said Spayte. "Thunstone, all you say is good to hear, since you seem to have escaped from something highly interesting. Now, as you say, the police are busy at that place called Chimney Pots. Even CID men, is that so? What have they found in that cave?"

"In the place where Gram was supposed to sleep his ten thousand years, they found ashes," said Thunstone. "Ashes and pieces of bone. The doctor they brought says the bone isn't human bone; he can't say what it is. They've sent for experts to decide."

"And Gram Ensley?" asked Spayte.

"He's just as Constable Dymock described him," replied Thunstone. "Seems to be smashed, as if he'd been hit by a truck."

"Then that image in the chalk up on the hillside," said Vickery. "It's gone—burnt out—fire, you said. What's left to research?"

"The scraps and splinters of the Dream Rock," said Thunstone. "Gates, the curate at St. Jude's, has gathered them carefully together. Maybe they can be fitted back into shape."

"I wonder if they should be," said Vickery. "Here, miss, bring me another mug of what this is. Thunstone, when you broke that rock up, you seem to have headed off whatever might have happened."

"Whatever might have happened," Spayte echoed him. "I wonder if we'll ever know. What could that Gonda woman tell us?"

"We'll have to wait until she talks," said Thunstone. "This morning, she told Constance Bailey she couldn't manage to come down to breakfast, but to bring her up two soft-boiled eggs and some toast and coffee and stewed fruit. I've been to her room at Chimney Pots and brought back two big suitcases of her things and put them in the hall for her, whenever she can come downstairs."

"And Chimney Pots is full of police," said Spayte. "Just what are they up to?"

"Ensley's servants, Mr. and Mrs. Sayle, are being questioned," said

N43

Thunstone. "They're completely unstrung, aren't much help. They only say that they've always obeyed Ensley's orders, that they were used to doing that without really understanding, and that they were pretty much afraid of him."

"Small blame to them," said Spayte. "Have you finished your lunch? I have, and I'm eager to go to that house and see those Stone Age murals Thunstone's been talking about. Why not go?"

"Why not?" said Thunstone.

They all rose and walked out into Trail Street.

## ABOUT THE AUTHOR

MANLY WADE WELLMAN has been writing award-winning tales of fantasy, horror, and science fiction since 1931. His many novels include *The Hanging Stones, The Lost and the Lurking, After Dark,* and *The Old Gods Waken.* In addition to his novels featuring adventurer John Thunstone, he is also the author of the highly acclaimed series of tales, told in the Southern idiom, of the wandering balladeer Silver John. Wellman has won the Gandalf Award for Lifetime Achievement from the World Fantasy Convention. He lives in Chapel Hill, North Carolina.